Saving Kat

by

Cassidee Meeks

Saving Kat

Cover Art by *Diana Carlile*

The Wild Rose Press, Inc.
PO Box 708
Adams Basin, NY 14410-0708
Visit us at www.thewildrosepress.com

Publishing History
First Edition, 2021
Trade Paperback ISBN 978-1-5092-3768-5
Digital ISBN 978-1-5092-3769-2

Published in the United States of America

"My cat and I do not see eye to eye. Especially when it concerns you. I often fight her for control when you are close, which is another reason I try to avoid you." Katrina sighed.

"I learned incredibly early as a child that the only way to keep myself under control was to analyze my feelings as if they were facts rather than emotions. We are taught to keep ourselves hidden from humans and to keep our animal under control, so we're not discovered, but I had such a hard time with my emotions. I felt everything so deeply that I had to leash my cat and sometimes disassociate from her—in order to keep her from becoming too much for me to handle. The more I tried to control her, the more feral she became. I struggled every day to ignore what she wanted…"

Katrina frowned in frustration. "It's so hard to explain…it was just easier for me to stay away from you, but she did not agree with that choice."

"She doesn't let you hide from your emotions." Seth nodded understandingly. "Logically you realize that isn't healthy for either of you…right?"

Katrina huffed. "If I don't, I'm an emotional wreck."

"Then be a wreck—with me, Kat. You can be yourself. I accept you exactly as you are."

Katrina winced. Seth was the only one she'd ever allowed to use that nickname, but he was also the only one she'd ever hid from. "You don't know what you're asking."

Dedication

Writing books is my passion, but I could never do it alone. Without my family supporting me, my friends beta reading my books, and my editor polishing them to perfection, they would all still be rough drafts locked away in my computer. I want to thank everyone who has helped me through this journey, and those who have read and will continue to read my stories. You all make the time and effort so worth it for me.

Chapter One

"How about it, Seth? Tonight, Nia's?" Seth shook his head. He glanced at his fellow runners, the men he worked tirelessly with to bring down the rogue shifters who threatened not only the human population but other shifters as well. These men were his friends—his family. His pride. He trusted each one of them to have his back, but there was one thing he did not partake with them. "No thanks."

Gossom, one of the newer rogue hunters assigned to their group, chuckled. "Why not? Got a hot date tonight?"

Luc, one of Seth's oldest friends, spoke up. He knew exactly why Seth refused to expel his energy through the willing women that plagued Nia's local watering hole. "Nah, Seth has a mate."

"No kidding?" Gossom's gaze grew wide. "Who?"

"The ice princess," teased Lennix, Luc's twin brother.

Gossom frowned. "You don't mean the Alpha's daughter?"

Seth scowled at his friends. "Don't talk about her that way."

Gossom held up his hands in defense. "My bad, man."

Seth could've defended her until his dying breath, and had tried on several occasions, but it wouldn't

1

matter what he said. They still thought of her the same way. Not because she was cold, but because she knew they had a connection, and instead of coming home from university years ago after graduation, she'd opted to remain in the city. Away from him. She came home occasionally to visit the pride and her family, but somehow her visits always coincided with one of Seth's missions, which meant he was away and hadn't seen her since the day she'd left. He missed her. She pretended he didn't exist. It was pure hell.

Instead of drowning his sorrows in a willing female body, however, he was determined to be a man she deserved. He didn't want there to be any loose ends if she ever did decide to come home to him. He stayed away from Nia's, and he bided his time, choosing instead to use his spare moments to train. He exercised his frustrations away at home on his weights, and wished her scent wasn't just as strong now in his mind as it had been the day he'd first met her. The quiet, blonde-haired, green-eyed bookworm had wanted nothing to do with a big dumb jock like Seth who'd started early training to be one of the pack's rogue hunters. He'd done okay in school, but of course, Katrina had excelled. She was too smart for him—too talented. He'd tried to get her attention, but she'd simply roll her eyes and walk away. He didn't blame her. What good was he to her? She was a genius on a keyboard, and he was...what? Good at taking a hit? A decent killer? She deserved more. He strived to be better.

Seth watched his friends head off toward the bar, but he kept his nose headed straight for his house located only a few doors down from her parents. He walked past their house every day, and not just because he was hoping to catch her at home, but because his own father spent a fair amount of time at their alpha's as the pride's beta and second in charge. Seth knew he'd be the next to step up if ever his father retired, and he wanted to be ready.

He was a few feet from passing her house when her scent hit him hard, forcing him to stumble to a halt outside her bedroom window.

On the front porch of her house, Seth's father and hers sat in two rocking chairs as if they'd already retired. There was a game of chess set up between them, and they were playing by porch light, as the sun had set hours earlier. But Seth knew they weren't simply playing a game. They discussed strategy.

"Hey, Seth," called Katrina's father.

Seth didn't hesitate. This man wasn't just his alpha. Someday he'd be his father-in-law. If Katrina ever decided to accept him.

"Sir?" Seth bound up the stairs like a seventeen-year-old kid ready to escort the man's pride and joy to prom.

"Why don't you take a couple weeks off?"

"Uh…" Seth glanced distractedly toward the front door of his alpha's house. She was so close.

"You and the guys have done good this month, and I don't have any new rogue sightings to go on right now. I'm thinking a little break is in order. It's nice to get out of the monotony of it once in a while. Wouldn't want my best runner to grow stale."

"Mhm." Seth nodded. What was he supposed to say? Did the alpha know his daughter was Seth's mate? He was sure the news had gotten back to him, but Seth had never actually told the man. What difference did it make? Katrina clearly wasn't interested.

"My girls are home for Thanksgiving for a couple weeks. It would be nice if I had some extra guys around to keep the rogues away—if you're interested?"

"Sure." Seth nodded. Was it just him or was the alpha putting him in the perfect position to get close to Katrina? "No problem."

"Maybe you can talk Katrina into moving home while you're at it," muttered the alpha.

Seth held his breath.

"Yeah, I know. Just trying to help you out, kid. She's my daughter, and I know how stubborn she can be." The alpha winked at Seth, who still hadn't found his voice.

"Besides, if I can't trust my best runner to protect my daughter, then who can I trust?" The alpha shrugged dismissively. "Go let Sammara know you're staying for dinner."

Seth nodded and without a word made his way across the porch and inside the house. He closed the door quietly behind him and considered his first move. He could smell her delicious cinnamon scent lingering in every corner, and his gums throbbed in response. His mouth was watering by the time he made it to the kitchen where he could hear the women puttering around, and it wasn't because of the delicious fried chicken Katrina's mother was making for dinner either.

He entered the kitchen and, without even trying, his gaze landed on the vision of his dreams. The girl who'd haunted so many of his nights. He couldn't take his eyes off her, even when her mother greeted him with a warm smile.

"Hello, Seth!"

Katrina glanced up suddenly, as if shocked to see him, and dropped the bowl of boiled potatoes she'd been mashing. Her gaze avoided his as she knelt beside the counter, trying in vain to save what remained of the potatoes.

****

No, no, no, NO! Katrina was nearly in humiliated tears as he crouched down next to her with a towel to help her mop up the mess she'd just made. Why did it have to be *him*? Of all the people to see her do something stupid, it had to be the one guy she needed to be at her best in front of.

With half the mashed potatoes in the bowl and the other half in the trash, she set what remained of the creamy mixture on the counter, where her mother promptly poured a bit of milk into the bowl as if nothing had happened.

Katrina continued stirring, her gaze on the bowl in front of her, not daring to make eye contact with the guy who made every nerve in her body come alive with just one glance.

"All right, dear. Show me your laptop now. I'm going to bake this chicken the rest of the way. We have a few minutes."

Katrina shoved the bowl of mashed potatoes farther onto the counter and out of her way and quickly retrieved her laptop from the bag she'd left sitting at the kitchen table. Without a word, she allowed her hair to fall over her face, hiding from the keen gaze of the man who watched her like a hawk. He didn't say a word. Thankfully! Which was the only reason she hadn't dropped her laptop as well. Seth had to know what he did to her. There was no way he could miss the way she avoided making eye contact with him at every opportunity.

She tried to focus on the keyboard in front of her, but it took Katrina more than a couple tries to log into the pack's financial records. Her fingers just wouldn't cooperate. Not with Seth Mourgent sitting so close watching her contently as if he had all the time in the world.

"What am I looking at?" asked Katrina's mother.

"Daddy hasn't made any big purchases, right?"

"Not lately. We texted you about the last one. Why?"

"If I ran this right—"

"And I'm sure you did," prompted her mother with a nod. "You always do."

Katrina frowned. "There's ten thousand dollars missing from the pride's finances."

"Missing where?"

"I don't know. It's just gone... I've been running diagnostics, and it isn't a glitch. I checked your computer earlier to make sure it wasn't my laptop—it's not. The transfer is untraceable, but it didn't use pride security, so I don't think it's one of us."

"You think it was hacked?"

Katrina exhaled a deep breath. "Yeah."

"By whom?"

"By whoever's spending our ten thousand dollars."

"But the pride is fine, even with the missing money...right?"

Katrina smirked confidently. "Of course, between the runners, Nia's bar, Dezra's real estate business, and my paintings, all the big earners are doing their part.

Everyone is contributing what they can. But a hit like that can go a long way for our members. It could be an addition onto someone's house, or a repair…if we take too many hits like that…"

"Then you'll just have to fix it so they can't do that." She patted Katrina's cheek lovingly. "I know you can do it."

"I already did. That's not the point. Don't you want to know who took the money?"

"I'm sure they needed the money more than we currently do," her mother said with a shrug. "But let's not give them another freebie, heh?"

"But with enough time, I can trace the transfer. I can figure out who is responsible."

Her mother nodded again. "And if that's what your dad wants you to do, then go for it. But if he says leave it alone, then leave it alone. I know how you are. Don't get it in your head to go after them, Katrina."

Katrina pouted. "Ten thousand dollars is a lot of money, Mom…"

"It's not worth your life."

"They'll never even know I figured it out!"

This time her mother shook her head, ignoring Katrina's plea. "And if they find out? You live alone in the city. Our reach does not extend within city limits. We rely on vigilantes to keep you safe. You know as well as I do what your father is going to say if you want to pursue this."

Katrina huffed, forgetting for an instant that Seth was sitting at the breakfast bar listening. He hadn't made a sound, but she knew he hadn't missed a single word either. She swung her gaze toward his and scowled as if it was his fault her mother wasn't budging. Katrina closed her laptop with a soft snick and turned her attention back toward her mother. "Fine, but whoever took it got through my firewall. We're not dealing with an amateur. Sooner or later, it's going to happen again."

"And I'm sure you will handle it then as well."

"But they might not be content with ten thousand. They could empty the account."

"Maybe…but this one isn't the only account we have. We will be fine."

"Okay, but shouldn't I close the account or something?"

"Try not to worry. If it happens again, we'll close the account. Besides, your dad will be calling a meeting tomorrow night. You can bring it up then. For now, I haven't seen you in months—you promised to show me your latest project."

Katrina glanced self-consciously at Seth, then rolled her eyes. If he didn't like her art, that was on him. Plenty of people enjoyed her talents and spent a lot of money to own one of her pieces. "Fine, but if we go broke—I warned you." She went back to her laptop bag and opened a second compartment where she withdrew a canvas roughly the same size as her laptop and laid it on the counter for her mother to critique.

"I didn't have space for this one in the gallery." Katrina took a seat in front of the canvas and stared up at her mother expectantly.

"I don't suppose I can hang this one up on the fridge," she mumbled with a gasp of awe. "This is beautiful, dear!" Sammara picked the canvas up off the counter and studied the incredibly detailed forest scene Katrina had painted. It was a familiar one where the pride liked to run within their alpha's territory, and coincidently, the last place Katrina had seen Seth before heading off to college ten years earlier. "I love it."

"Good, because it's yours. I don't paint anything regarding the pride for sale. That one was for you. If you wanna see the rest, you have to go to the website."

"Would you mind going down to the basement and grabbing the pies I made earlier? I put them on the deep freeze to cool so they wouldn't be in the way. Your sister should be here any minute, and she's bringing a guest. Seth can help you."

Katrina would've loved to assure her mother that she didn't need Seth's help, but before she could open her mouth to respond, he was already on his feet, through the living room, and heading for the basement door. Instead, she sent her mother a frustrated look and forced herself to follow the man she'd been fantasizing about since puberty.

"You paint?" Seth stood beside the deep freezer, studying the pies her mother had sent them after.

"I took an art class and found I had a talent for painting. Who would have thought?"

"You have a lot of talents. I'm not surprised."

Was that a compliment? Katrina couldn't tell. It sounded forced to her untrained ear. "Is there a reason you're here? In my parents' house, I mean?"

He smirked. "It isn't obvious?"

"Not really."

"I tried throughout our entire childhood to get your attention, then you left and made it abundantly clear that you didn't want me to bother you. I haven't seen you in ten years...you know exactly why I'm here."

Katrina flinched. "To taunt me?"

Seth lifted his gaze toward hers. "Taunt you? When did I ever?"

"I don't want to talk about this. Let's just get the damned pies." Katrina stalked toward him, intent on grabbing one of the desserts, but he latched onto her wrist and pulled her in close before she could reach the deep freezer.

"Too bad. I've waited a long time to talk to you. You can spare a minute."

Katrina felt all the breath leave her body as his fingers touched her skin. He'd only ever touched her one other time, and the contact had been enough to ruin her for anyone else. His touch was the only one she craved.

"What did I do to you that was so wrong that you'd rather hide out in the city than risk seeing me? Don't think I haven't noticed that you only come home while I'm gone. You plan it that way. I know you do."

"So?"

"But why?"

Katrina inhaled a deep breath, hoping to shake the heat that had settled in the pit of her stomach with his touch. "Because you…you…you frustrate me!" She made a half-hearted attempt to pull away, and he let her go.

"Because I try to talk to you?"

She couldn't stop from rolling her eyes. "Every day at lunch, for a year, you and your stupid friends thought it was funny to distract me from my studies. I'd sit there minding my own business, and you'd try your best to tease me until I had no choice but to get up and move to another seat.

"And it wasn't just that. You'd throw crumbled

balls of paper at me in class, and then your friends would laugh even more. It's hard enough being the alpha's daughter with all these expectations, and you just made it all the more difficult than it already was, and you knew these bonds would make sure I had no choice but to pay attention to you."

"First of all, I wasn't trying to distract you from anything," hissed Seth. "I was trying to get your attention because I liked you. My friends weren't laughing at you, they were laughing at my failed attempts to get your attention. And if you'd ever bothered to read any of the balls of paper I tossed in your direction, you'd have known that. Admittedly, I was a hormonal teenager and desperate to get you to realize I existed, but nothing I did was meant to hurt you."

Katrina swallowed. Surely, she hadn't been so wrong all these years. "All you had to do was say you liked me—you didn't have to pick on me."

"I didn't! Not on purpose. I'm obviously bad at flirting, but I honestly just wanted to spend time with you. I couldn't just tell you I liked you. I didn't think you'd take me seriously."

"And you thought repeatedly poking me in the arm with your pencil while we were supposed to be studying was a better method?" Katrina rolled her eyes once more.

"See! That! Every time I talk to you, you do that!" Seth huffed. "I don't know how to respond to that."

"Well, see it from my point of view. I'm not the prettiest girl in the pride. I know that. I didn't socialize with the others. I didn't have friends. And I spent ninety percent of my time with my nose in a book. You were this adorable, funny guy who was friends with everyone. I was not your type."

Seth stared at her in shock. "The fact that you honestly believe that blows my mind. You are beautiful! And how the hell would you know what my type is when you wouldn't give five minutes to get to know me? You don't know anything about me!"

"The fact that you don't see that we're total opposites blows my mind."

"Right. You're the smart, pretty girl, and I'm the dumb jock who's only talent is taking a hit. Got it. I must've forgotten my place."

Katrina watched in stunned disbelief as he picked up one of the pies and left her standing alone in the basement with the other. She stared after him, his words piercing the fog that clouded her mind each time he looked at her. She hadn't expected him to be so angry at her, even if she'd been avoiding him for the last decade. It wasn't as if they were officially mated. Seth could be with any girl he wanted. Katrina snatched up the second dessert and headed for the stairs, her mind spinning a mile a minute as she made it to the kitchen to place her pie next to his on the counter.

Her mother was no longer cooking and must've been outside on the porch, because Katrina could hear their voices, though not what they said through the soundproof walls her father had built into their house.

Seth seemed to be heading for the front door, but Katrina couldn't let him leave believing his version of what she thought of him. It wasn't fair.

"I never said that," hissed Katrina, not wanting her parents to hear.

Seth paused and spun back toward Katrina,

heading in her direction as if she'd just insulted him. "What is the opposite of smart and pretty, then, Katrina? Because maybe I'm too stupid to understand."

"Those were your words, not mine. I said you were adorable and funny."

He hesitated. "I realize I'm not good enough for you—"

"I never said that either." Katrina scowled, too frustrated with his lack of confidence to care if she admitted the truth.

"Then why won't you talk to me? It's been so long, and you still avoid me."

"You are scary. You represent everything in life that I can't handle. You go out with the pride, you have friends, and females practically drool all over you. You are my father's pride and joy hunter, the son my father wishes he had. Nothing I do will ever compare. I can't be that girl."

"What girl?" Seth groaned. "What part of me don't you want?"

Katrina hesitated. He sounded so vulnerable. She'd never known him to be anything but laughing and happy. The thought that she'd hurt him was unbearable. He was her mate, and every instinct in her body insisted that she make this right. "I'm not the girl you can be happy with. I'm never going to want to go out with your friends and get drunk at Nia's. I'm not going to compete with other women for your attention or learn to hunt rogues. I can only be what I already am."

"Which is exactly what I want you to be." His voice lowered as he moved closer to her. "There are no other women you need to worry about, and I don't drink. Frankly, the idea of you hunting rogues terrifies me. I just…" He hesitated.

"What," breathed Katrina, unable to keep the hope from her voice. "You just what?"

"Want you to acknowledge that I exist. Tell me I'm not the only one who feels these bonds. You're all I think about, Katrina. I'm losing my mind."

He was telling the truth. His scent called to her and dared her to deny his words. She'd avoided him for so long believing that he'd used their bonds to tease her, but she'd been wrong. Seth deserved better than what she'd given him. She deserved better than what she'd offered herself.

"You know," began Katrina carefully, "I don't actually like living in the city…If I came home, we could discuss this mating thing."

"You've only been living in the city to avoid me?" He looked hurt.

"To avoid what you do to me."

"The same thing you do to me," muttered Seth.

Katrina stared at him, the way his bright golden eyes focused on her as if she were the only girl in the world. She longed to run her fingers through his thick, long tresses and pull his face down toward hers. She wanted to kiss him, but more than that, she wanted to wrap her arms around him and never let go.

The mating bonds were a helluva thing, but even more so when his scent called to her, begging her to take a bite. Katrina's gums throbbed, his feline scent luring her like a moth to a flame, insisting she curl up in his arms and purr until he understood what she needed.

She stared up at him wishing she could say all the things she'd longed to say since the moment she'd met him at only thirteen years old, when he'd offered that boyish grin, and her heart had felt the stirrings of an innocent first love. From that moment on, she'd held a soft spot for him in her heart, that even when she felt he'd used their bonds to entertain his friends, she could still never stay mad at him.

It had seemed so unfair at the time, and she'd decided to even the playing field by simply staying away from him, but it hadn't been what she'd wanted, and apparently he hadn't either. So what was she supposed to do now? Tell him the truth? She opened her mouth to do just that when she heard the front door open and her parents' voices growing louder as they entered the house.

Seth sent her a meaningful look just as Katrina's mother entered the kitchen. "Seth, honey, won't you stay for dinner? Dezra is bringing home a friend, and we won't have enough people to play teams for family game night if you leave."

Seth glanced at Katrina questioningly.

Katrina nodded. "You should stay, I'm terrible at games."

"Someone as good at numbers as you? I would've thought you'd be great!" He grinned at her response.

"I'm not good at numbers. I'm terrible at math. I'm good at computers, and with the correct information, a computer can tell you anything. The pride finances are relatively easy to handle considering my father records every single penny. Which is why I noticed the missing money so easily. I'm good at graphic design and art, but you can't win anything but Pictionary with decent drawing skills. I'm actually super bad at reading people, which is why I'm terrible at games."

Seth smirked. "I would love to stay for dinner,

Mrs. Valenthia, and I'd be honored to be Katrina's partner for the night. Besides, I have it on good authority that Dezra's friend might be more than that, and I'm curious to see the guy who thinks he can handle her."

Her mother chuckled. "Me too, sweetie. Set an extra place at the table. Show him where the good dishes are, Katrina."

Katrina rolled her eyes with a grin and led Seth into the dining room, where her mother had set only four places. "The plates are in that cabinet." She pointed at the china hutch where her mother kept the *good* dishes for guests. "I'll grab some napkins and silverware." Katrina's body burned when Seth's gaze stayed on her the entire time as she wrapped the silverware set in the cotton napkins her mother preferred.

"Look," she whispered, hoping her mother's ever-listening ears wouldn't hear her words. "I'm interested in figuring out this mating thing, but you've got to stop looking at me like that when my parents are in the room. I can't focus."

"Like what," purred Seth with a half-lidded gaze that said he knew exactly what she was talking about.

"Like I'm naked," she hissed.

He grinned. "I can't help myself. I've never been so close to you for this long without you rolling your eyes or running away from me. You make me want you."

"Well…want me a little bit less."

"Kiss me, and I'll try."

Katrina rolled her eyes once more, sure that one day her eyes were going to roll right back into her head and never come out again. It was her signature move—her only move, and she used it any time she needed to avoid an awkward situation much like this one. She set the last piece of silverware next to the plate he'd just placed and crossed her arms. "And what good will kissing do?"

His grin widened. "Let me find out."

"Fine." She closed her eyes.

Seth chuckled, but she felt him lean closer. She held her breath, waiting, but he merely nuzzled her cheek with his, mixing his scent with hers, combining a potent mix that made her turn her face toward him, seeking to press her mouth against his.

He held perfectly still, and their lips met, cementing what she'd known all along. Seth was her mate. How had she ever thought she could simply stay away from him?

Katrina leaned closer and lifted her arms around his neck, needing more than a mere touch of his mouth to soothe her aching heart. She'd thought of him and what he'd taste like, but nothing could've prepared her for the sugary warm taste of freshly baked cinnamon rolls, as if he were all the damned dessert she'd ever need. She moaned at the deliciousness of him and sought to deepen the kiss.

He complied without hesitation, and his hands found their way to her hips, drawing her even closer, until her entire body was flush against his, absorbing his heat, imprinting the feel of him on her skin. He was everything she'd ever imagined he'd be, but he was so much more than she'd thought too.

"Finally!"

Katrina flinched as her sister's voice interrupted

her thoughts and the kiss. She'd been so absorbed in his touch she'd failed to notice her sister's own personal scent filling the room. Katrina untangled herself from Seth's grip and straightened her T-shirt as if it were wrinkled. Her nose turned defensively in the air momentarily before she cleared her throat and refused to look at anything but the tablecloth her mother had chosen for the night.

Dezra giggled. "Klyn, this is my sister Katrina and her mate Seth. I've been waiting for this moment my whole life."

"Not your whole life," protested Katrina, sure that her sister was exaggerating.

"I was *eleven* when you started drawing little hearts around his name. That's practically my whole life," protested Dezra.

Seth grinned. "Really?"

"Thanks, Dezra. If it wasn't clear how socially awkward I was before, it is now." Katrina offered her sister's friend a greeting. "To be fair, I've known he was my mate since I was thirteen. I feel like I was entitled to a few doodles once in a while."

Klyn nodded, a friendly grin on his face as he chuckled. "I agree. I'd be more surprised if you didn't. I mean—thirteen is a hard age, anyway. Throw in a life partner, and it's bound to be difficult."

"Since we're divulging embarrassing childhood stories, you'll have to ask Dezra about her rock collection."

"Let's not," huffed Dezra with a playful scowl in Katrina's direction.

"Now I have to know," laughed Klyn.

"Does this have anything to do with you getting in

trouble for throwing rocks at people all the time," asked Seth with a raised eyebrow.

Dezra groaned. "I used to throw rocks at boys I thought were cute…then I'd keep the rock I threw at them like a souvenir. But I never doodled secret pictures of my sort of boyfriend."

Katrina grinned then. "Okay, A—I didn't doodle any pictures of him, I painted one picture, and it was of his cat, it hardly counts. And B—what exactly is a *sort of* boyfriend? Is that like a *sort of* mate?" She smirked at Dezra's wide-eyed grin.

"Yes, it's the exact same," laughed Klyn. "Am I the sort of mate in this scenario," whispered Klyn in Dezra's direction.

Dezra exhaled. "Well, if she's just gonna out me like that!" She grinned then. "I missed you. Why haven't you come home sooner?"

"I've been pretending like I don't have a sort of boyfriend." Katrina shrugged as if it wasn't a big deal.

"Well, are you done yet?" Dezra's gaze was filled with hope.

"I sure as hell hope so," muttered Seth beneath his breath.

Katrina couldn't stop herself from focusing on Seth as she spoke. "You'd probably follow me home at this point anyway. I might as well."

"Your dad did give me a couple of weeks off." Seth shrugged.

"You work for her dad?" asked Klyn curiously. "How does that work?"

Chapter Two

Seth couldn't believe what he was hearing. Just hours earlier, he was prepared to go home and take his frustrations out on the exercise equipment he'd invested in, but now he was in Katrina's home, inhaling her scent, talking to her! He'd touched her, kissed her, and now she was acknowledging their bonds in ways he'd only ever dreamt of! It didn't seem real. He'd imagined this moment hundreds of times, but it had never compared to this! She was smiling at him, joking with him, and yes—still rolling her eyes at him, but damned if he didn't suddenly think it was the cutest thing he'd ever seen. If only he'd learned to read her sooner!

"I've been training to be a runner since high school. I had a lot of time on my hands. My dad is the alpha's beta, so it works out pretty well," admitted Seth with a shrug. The last thing Seth wanted to be discussing was his job, but short of pulling Katrina away from her family and further exploring their mating bonds in the privacy of his own home, he couldn't very well ignore a potential new member of the pride. As the alpha's lead runner, it was his job to know everyone.

"Is he looking for more runners?" asked Klyn casually.

"Always. Rogues are a constant threat. Are you a runner?"

"I was…my brother and I did free-lance, but he met his mate and, now that she's pregnant, he's not as keen on chasing bad guys. I'm only a half breed though. Is that a problem?"

"Nah, I'm only a half breed. My mother is human. It's not a big deal. Our alpha doesn't much care about that sort of thing. But you'll have to put in an official request with him, and he'll want you to swear loyalty. Since you're mating his daughter though, I assume you already knew that was coming."

Klyn nodded. "I considered as much."

"And?" Seth studied the new male.

"Oh—of course! I was raised by my father's family, so I don't have a pride. My brother and I never even knew about the jaguar thing until we hit puberty, and we ended up running away from home thinking something was wrong with us. It wasn't until years later that we met up with others like us and figured it out. We've been on our own, just the two of us since."

"You'd be surprised how often that happens…my mother chose to give up her former life to stay with my father and without any connections to her human side, our alpha is confident that she can be trusted. We were lucky. It usually doesn't happen that way." For a long while, Seth thought maybe his muddy DNA had been the reason Katrina hadn't liked him, but then he'd realized it wasn't just him she avoided, but everyone— pure and hybrid alike.

Seth was about to explain what exactly a pride runner did when he heard his alpha's voice as Ward entered the kitchen from the porch. The scent of Seth's own father was fading, and he assumed that meant their chess game was over and dinner would start soon.

Sure enough, Sammara, his alpha's mate, entered the room carting a tray full of fried chicken. Behind her, their alpha followed with a serving tray of various dishes, including the mashed potatoes Katrina had massacred.

"Sit, sit! Make yourself at home," insisted Sammara with a wide, welcoming grin. She took a seat next to the head of the table where the alpha then took his seat.

"It's good to see you girls home," spoke up Ward, though his voice held a tone of reproach.

Seth immediately moved to hold Katrina's chair away from the table for her. He wanted to show her and everyone else that he was serious about this mating thing, starting now. He waited for her to take her seat, then carefully sat in the chair next to her, claiming his spot at her side.

"I expect you'll be here more than a day or two this time," added Ward with a glint in his eye as his gaze circled the table.

Seth kept his mouth firmly shut. He wanted to hear Katrina's official answer as much as her father apparently did.

Dezra spoke first, however. "Daddy, this is Klyn. He's my mate," she announced proudly, and her hand found his and held it over the table.

Seth longed for Katrina to do the same thing, but he doubted she would. She and her sister were as different as night and day. A little acknowledgement of their bonds would go a long way in his book, though.

"I suspected. What pride are you from? I can smell the cat on you," said Ward confidently as Sammara began passing around the various dishes.

"I don't know. My mother didn't stick around long after my brother and I were born. It's just been us for a while," explained Klyn for the second time that night.

Ward nodded. "And how do you feel about joining a clan—officially?"

"Hesitant, but willing to do whatever it takes to make your daughter happy."

Seth wished he'd said something like that as well, but he'd only ever pined Katrina's absence and wished she'd give him the time of day. It might've helped if he'd told Ward the truth, but he'd assumed his alpha wouldn't want his daughter mated to Seth any more than Katrina had seemed to.

"Glad to hear it." Ward nodded his approval and switched his attention toward Katrina. "And how long do you plan to stick around this time?"

Katrina flinched, and Seth wanted to scoop her up in his arms and guard her from the world. This protective streak wasn't a new thing for him, but it was something he'd never been able to act on before.

"I've decided to move back home," announced Katrina quietly, her gaze carefully avoiding everyone else's.

Seth couldn't take it anymore. He reached beneath the table where he was sure no one would see and gave her hand an encouraging squeeze. He'd never been able to be there for her before, but he intended to take every opportunity to support her in whatever way she needed him to. As her mate, he saw it as his personal duty to be whatever she needed him to be.

Sammara gasped and nearly dropped the same mashed potato bowl Katrina had earlier. "What?" Her gaze widened excitedly. "You are? When?"

"As soon as I can find somewhere to put my stuff." Katrina shrugged as if she hadn't just said the one thing her parents had been hoping for since the day she first left for college. "I don't exactly want to move back in with my parents."

Seth bit his tongue. He had a perfect place she could put her things, but he couldn't offer his house to her just yet. Not before she told her parents the truth. It didn't matter that her father already knew. Katrina had to say it out loud.

"What made you decide to come home?" teased Dezra with a knowing grin.

Katrina sent her sister a scowl. "I'm thinking of taking over the local real-estate industry," she taunted, referring to her sister's booming business, but it was a lie. It didn't make it any less amusing to Seth, however. He grinned, unable to help himself. He'd never heard Katrina's sense of humor before, but he thought he might like it. She seemed to have a sarcastic bite that was right up his alley.

"Are you having problems with the locals in the city, Katrina?" demanded Ward.

"They've been perfectly nice. It has nothing to do with that." Katrina sighed. "I've just realized some things and think it's time to come home."

"What things?" asked Dezra slyly.

Seth held his breath.

Katrina lifted her gaze and squared her shoulders. "The truth?"

"If this is about the money—" interrupted Sammara.

"What money?" gasped Dezra. "Do you need money?"

"Money?" asked Ward with a frown.

"It's not, Mom. And no, Dezra, I don't. We can talk about it later." Seth could hear Katrina tapping her toe on the floor nervously, and he did his best to keep her calm with his thumb, tracing little circles on the back of her hand. He hoped his small show of support was having the desired effect. Their bond wasn't deep enough for him to tell yet.

"Oh…are you okay, dear?" Sammara frowned. "You seem…anxious. What's got you so upset?"

"Katrina?" Ward's voice was filled with concern. "What's wrong?"

"I…" Katrina's gaze filled with tears as she struggled to speak.

There was no way she was going to mention him, decided Seth. It wasn't possible their connection could move her to tears.

"Katrina?" Even Dezra's voice held an inkling of unease. "You're not pregnant, are you?"

Seth could have cried. Surely not. He prayed to every deity he'd ever heard of that his mate wasn't carrying someone else's child. He'd never considered that she might have a boyfriend somewhere. Mate or not, they weren't yet bonded. She could've taken a lover. She could be pregnant. His heart hurt to consider it, but he kept a careful lid on his emotions. It didn't matter. His child or not, if she agreed to be his mate, he'd raise the baby as his own.

"I just missed my mate, and I feel so stupid because I didn't want to admit I did," gasped Katrina with a groan.

The whole room fell silent.

Seth was dead. There was no other way he could

describe the euphoria he felt. He'd died and gone to whatever Heaven must exist, because there was no way she'd actually said those words.

"Honey..." Sammara smiled encouragingly. "You were gone from him for ten years...it's natural..."

Katrina rolled her eyes, and Seth was glad it wasn't directed at him for once.

"Yes, but it doesn't make sense! I don't even know him. What exactly am I missing? We're not bonded technically. Is it his scent? I need to know what exactly I missed about him."

Dezra snorted. "Stop thinking about it like a science experiment. There are no chemicals affecting your brain."

"That's not technically true," countered Klyn. "There are plenty of chemicals involved, but none she would've experienced after so many years and from a distance. The lack of his scent would surely have affected her for the first year or so, but if there was no bite, or..." He cleared his throat shyly. "Uh, mating, that would imply that you simply missed him as a person. Whether you know someone or not, if you spent a lot of time together, then he was a part of your life in whatever regard, and you missed his presence."

Katrina frowned thoughtfully, and Seth felt like his heart was going to beat right out of his chest.

"That makes sense...We went to school together, so I saw him every single day. I never really talked to him, but I saw him. A lot." Katrina huffed. "We had most of the same classes together...and I've known him since I was thirteen, so that's—" she paused "—five years of constant interaction."

"Well, yeah, but we've known each other our

whole lives, and you didn't miss me," growled Dezra. "And we've only seen each other at holidays, so it must be more than that."

"You're an excellent cook, Mom," Katrina blurted out suddenly.

Seth wasn't sure what was happening or why she quickly changed the subject, but he was fairly certain it was in his favor.

"You said something about money," growled Ward, his focus evidently more directed toward the pride finances than his daughter's confusion on the mechanics of shifter mating mannerisms.

Katrina's gaze widened, and she latched onto her father's change of topic with obvious relief. "Yes! I did!"

Seth felt her turn her hand over and weave her fingers between his. He didn't realize he could be any happier in that moment, but one simple touch had set his pulse on fire. It was in that instant, holding her hand beneath the table, that he realized the only possible truth. He loved her. There was no way it was simply their mating bonds that had affected him all these years. He knew almost nothing about her, but he'd known her for so long, had craved her attention from the moment he'd met her, and now that he had it, he could never go back. If she left again, he knew he'd follow her, and not even his alpha would be able to stop him. He needed her as much as he needed his next breath.

"And?" Prompted Ward expectantly.

"We're missing ten thousand dollars," admitted Katrina.

Seth tried his best to follow the conversation, but having heard most of it earlier, he could hardly focus on much more than the feel of her skin on his as he devoured his dinner. He was silent, absorbing the energy he felt buzzing between them, gorging himself on the heat of her flesh pressed against his. He'd never felt so close to her in his entire life!

****

"What?" gasped Dezra, startling Katrina as she waited for her father to acknowledge her words.

Klyn choked on his glass of water. "Did you say ten thousand?"

It didn't seem to be the greatest idea in Katrina's mind to let the newest member of their family in on their financial situation just yet, even if he was Dezra's mate. They didn't know a thing about him. But no one other than Katrina seemed to mind that he was present for the conversation, and who was she to decide who was allowed to know and who wasn't? Not the alpha—that's who.

Katrina breathed a sigh of relief as Seth closed his palm around hers. This was the moment she'd thirsted for as a teenager. She'd wished upon every star she'd seen that he would take her hand in his and hold it as if she were more than his mate. She'd wanted to be his girlfriend, and she hadn't cared what anyone else thought. At least, she hadn't until she'd felt like he was abusing their bonds for the amusement of their peers with his immature antics.

Now that she knew the truth, she wished she'd been a little less reluctant to respond to him. Maybe if she'd said something instead of walking away her entire life would be different. Katrina tried not to think about all the wasted time she'd spent hurt and angry at him, hiding miles away from him as if she could pretend he didn't exist. It hadn't accomplished anything.

Instead, she opened herself to the possibility of now and held Seth's hand beneath the table as if she couldn't bear to let go. In truth, she couldn't. His touch was like a warm balm on her touch-starved skin. She was addicted. One touch, and already she couldn't imagine letting him go ever again. It was ridiculous, but it felt so right.

When no one else said a word, she decided to add to her previous account.

"It isn't marked, and I can't trace the transfer. My firewall was breached. I've built up my firewall and plugged any entrance into the site, so it shouldn't happen again. If it does, they're smarter than me, and we should close the account before they clean us out," advised Katrina.

"You're just going to let them steal ten thousand dollars from you?" gasped Klyn in shock.

"I'm not letting them," protested Katrina. "I was forbidden from pursuing it whilst residing outside pride territory."

"But you're moving home," protested Dezra.

"And I've been convinced that it is in my best interest to let it go. We can afford to lose it, and besides, I have other things to focus my time on just now." Katrina shrugged. She wasn't a bit ashamed that she'd rather spend her time getting to know her mate than tracking a thief. Especially because her mother had made the choice for her.

"Let's transfer most of the money from the account and leave a small sum for our thieves to find. I know you can embed some sort of tracker or virus that will allow us to figure out who is robbing our pride. You will not pursue the thief, but you may work with our lead tracker to find out who it is and bring it to my attention," announced Ward.

"And your lead tracker is?"

"Me." Seth grinned. "Welcome to the team."

"Team?" echoed Katrina, already fearing the worst.

"No one hunts alone," confessed Ward with a shrug. "Not even the best. Seth heads team one. You can join them, but not on a physical hunt. Seth is your mate. I trust him with your care. You are not to set foot in the field. Am I understood?"

"I'm not trained," huffed Katrina. "Of course, I'm not going in the field!" Her heart raced at the mere thought, but even as she began to calm herself, another unwanted thought intruded. Seth was in the field all the time. He was constantly in danger. At any time in the last ten years he could've been killed. She could have lost her mate. Her heart sank. Her father said he was the best, but she needed to see for herself.

"They usually deal with rogues, right? How do they fare against someone in their right mind who's simply an asshole? Or just desperate?"

"Runners are trained to think on their feet. It's more than physical training," insisted Dezra.

Katrina scowled. "I *never* said they weren't smart!" She tightened her grip on Seth's hand, assuring him that she did *not* think he was any less intelligent than her. "I just want to be sure we know what we're up against before they go after the thief."

Dezra's gaze widened. "That's not what I meant, Katrina."

Katrina scowled down at her half-eaten dinner. "I never said they were stupid," she muttered insistently.

Seth squeezed her hand briefly, and she managed to turn her gaze toward his. He smiled, and her racing heart calmed a fraction. There had to be some type of chemical responsible for his ability to affect her so easily. It couldn't simply be his presence. It couldn't just be their connection. Surely.

She smiled back at him in relief. "It's likely the thief isn't a rogue. They're probably in perfect order of their senses. It's too hard to hack a bank account. A rogue shouldn't be able to process the information fast enough to get through a firewall without setting off any alarms. I got a notification that there'd been a withdrawal, but there was no password login notification in my email. I have all the settings turned on. Nothing but the withdrawal showed up on my phone. I checked the accounts. Only the newest one was hit, and they didn't take it all. The person is probably just desperate, or they would've emptied the account. I don't think we're dealing with someone evil. Whoever took the money is smart, but they might need our help. I'm less inclined to believe it's someone that needs to be killed but instead someone we need to rescue. Can the runners do that?" She kept her attention on Seth now, wanting him to be the one to answer.

Seth's eyes flashed, and he grinned. "Absolutely."

Katrina nodded and turned her attention back toward her father. "Do we have permission for that?"

"Once we see who the thief is, we'll proceed. Until then, we need to maintain that they are dangerous. Your runners are trained to handle any situation you throw at them, but let's not test their abilities until we know for sure."

"Honey—" interrupted her mother. She patted her

mate's hand lovingly. "Let's not do this yet."

"Do what?" demanded Dezra. "Why did you call them her runners?"

This time her mother sighed. "We've known for quite some time that Seth is Katrina's mate. Probably as long as they've known. We wanted to wait until she told us, but when it seemed like she wouldn't, our plans went in a different direction. But I think we should wait to mention it. Katrina has only just decided to move home. She needs time to readjust first."

Katrina inhaled a deep breath. "You might as well tell me now. I'm not going anywhere."

Her parents stared at her thoughtfully. "You're certain?"

Katrina lifted her hand, showing Seth's firmly attached to hers. "Positive."

Her mother and father glanced at one another, then nodded.

"I've decided it's time to consider a new alpha—just in case," announced Ward.

"Why? What's wrong?" gasped Dezra, her dark green eyes shining with unshed tears. "Are you sick? Hurt?"

"No, no, nothing like that. It's just time to consider a replacement in case something happens. All prides have an alternative alpha waiting to take care of the pride should something happen. Neither you nor your sister have the alpha tendencies required to lead the pride. I'm sure either one of you could step up and do it if you had to, but we already have someone in the pride who could do it now. I've been discussing it with my council…"

Katrina stared at her father; she could guess what

he was about to say.

Her mother smiled encouragingly. "Go on."

Ward nodded. "Seth…your father and I have discussed this at length for a while now. I worried with Katrina gone that it might not be the best idea, but we believe you can step up when the time comes. Even while she was gone, you've proven your character to be in her best interest. I've watched you for a long time, and I feel like you can lead our pride as well as I have, if not better. When I do step down, I'd like you to consider taking my place."

Katrina held her breath. For Seth, she knew this was the highest possible honor. For herself, she would've never accepted such a position of responsibility over so many people. Seth could do it, though. She wasn't sure how she knew that, since she'd never given him a chance to prove himself, but something in her believed in him.

"Sir…" Seth's palm grew sweaty in hers.

"Wait, before you answer." Katrina licked her lips nervously. "Can I talk to him before he answers?"

"Absolutely. This isn't something he should decide without talking to you first. You are partners. You should do everything together," agreed her mother. "And we don't need an answer tonight, anyway. It's just something to think about."

"When you said her runners, you meant because Seth is her mate. He's our top runner," said Dezra carefully. "As his mate, he would listen to her above even his alpha. He's already head of your security, so you'd either have to fire him, promote him to beta, or…alpha."

"I already have the best beta I could ask for. What I

33

don't have is an alpha to take my place, and Seth's father doesn't want—nor would he be the best man for the position. We've put a lot of thought into this, and our council agrees. Seth would make an excellent alpha."

Katrina felt the same certainty her father expressed deep in her soul. She stood suddenly, dragging Seth to his feet beside her. "Let's skip game night tonight."

"You were going to lose anyway," teased Dezra with a grin.

"Exactly. And I need to get started on tracking our thief. I'll make it up to you guys. There will be plenty of time for game nights once I'm home for good." Katrina spewed as many excuses as she could possibly think of on the fly, then tugged Seth away from the table and toward the front door.

"Take me to your house," she whispered, her pulse racing. It didn't matter what he thought was about to happen. Regardless of what might actually occur, they needed to talk.

Seth didn't say a word but led her out of the house and then farther down the street, past his own parents' house, and farther still, until he reached a small two-bedroom split level. The door wasn't locked, as was common for shifters living confidently within the pride boundaries. He led her inside without hesitation then up the stairs where he suddenly froze in the middle of what she assumed was his living room and stood staring at his couch, as if it might come alive and attack him.

Katrina didn't need to be told what he was feeling. She had a heightened sense of reluctance flooding her too and knew he must be feeling at least a fraction of that same thing, if not hundreds of other emotions. She needed him to know she wasn't something he should worry about in this equation. Above all else, she wanted him to be confident in their relationship—whatever it may be. She wouldn't be leaving him again. Not willingly.

"Sit with me," she said gently, and she tugged him toward the couch, where she pulled him down beside her.

Seth didn't respond out loud but let her lead him.

Katrina lifted his arm around her shoulder and snuggled up beneath his grip, her head on his chest, listening to the rapid beating of his heart as they sat in companionable silence. She watched the clock tick on the wall opposite of them until she began to feel at ease with the sound of his heart beating beneath her ear.

Chapter Three

Seth was in shock. Or at least, he had been for the first five minutes. But as Katrina began to purr in his arms, thoughts of leading the pride as their new alpha faded to shock of another kind entirely. Katrina was in his arms. Her head was on his chest. She was purring! He couldn't keep his heart from trying to rip itself from his chest, and he knew she most likely assumed it was the thought of leading the pride that had him nearly hyperventilating, but it wasn't.

The instant Ward had called the runners Katrina's, Seth had immediately assumed that his next words would be Seth's invitation as alpha. He was obviously shocked, but not nearly as much as he would've been if Katrina hadn't been home. Katrina. Seth's mate was FINALLY home. After so long of wishing, hoping, and praying that she'd come back, she was home, and she was in his arms. He kept thinking it must be a dream, but as she curled up next to him, his entire body burned with pure delight. His mate was home, where she belonged. With him.

The guys had called her an ice princess, but they had no clue who she really was. Katrina wasn't cold. She was calculating, maybe, with her ability to coincide her visits with his absences, but she wasn't the frigid beauty they'd assumed she was. The distance between them was only partially her fault, and Seth wanted to make sure everyone knew that Katrina wasn't solely to blame. But first, he held her as if ten years of craving her attention hadn't made him desperate. Because he felt desperate. He loved her, and she was finally exactly where she belonged. His heart was beating so hard he was sure it would keep her awake, but then her purring had faded, and he knew she'd fallen asleep in his arms.

It was a dream come true. Katrina, his beautiful, smart, future mate was in his arms, sleeping as if she trusted him! He knew it was too much to hope, but he couldn't keep his cat from purring. She owned them, heart and soul. Soon enough she'd know it too but, until then, he was going to do everything in his power to show her exactly what she meant to him. There would be no more misunderstandings. From now on he was going to say precisely what he meant. He couldn't risk losing her ever again.

Seth held her a little tighter and slid down next to her, pulling her body against his until they lay side by side on the plush oversized couch. His bed would've been preferable, but he'd never been more comfortable in his entire life. He only hoped she'd be as affectionate in the morning when she woke up beside him and realized he wasn't thinking nearly as hard about being the next alpha as he was about being with her.

****

Katrina didn't dare move. Somehow she'd found herself tucked into Seth's arms as if it were the most natural thing in the entire world. She'd been awake for almost an hour and had had to pee for nearly the entire time, but she refused to so much as breathe too deeply for fear of waking him. She stared up at his face, noting the gentle sweep of his lashes as the thick dark fringes brushed against his cheeks angelically, and was struck with the thought that she hoped all her future children had his lashes.

Shocked by the unexpected image, she flinched and unintentionally tossed herself out of his arms and onto the floor, where she smacked her elbow on the coffee table.

"What's wrong? Are you okay?" He was suddenly wide awake and staring down at her as if they'd been attacked. He glanced around, his expression ready and alert to take on anyone who might dare threaten them, then focused on her once more. "What happened?"

"I fell," mumbled Katrina, loath to admit the truth.

He raised one eyebrow as if he sensed her little white lie. "Did I push you?"

"No." Katrina inhaled a deep breath. "How does this work, exactly? I don't want to go back to the way we were. I can't help but try and analyze this as if it's an experiment I can solve, but logically I realize that's not how it works. You are better at this than me, so tell me what I'm supposed to do. My brain simply does not function when you're too close."

Seth grinned. He held out his hand to her and helped her back onto the couch next to him. "Start by telling me why you suddenly would rather throw yourself to the floor than lay next to me. The truth this time."

"Why?"

"Because honesty and communication are the key to any healthy relationship, and our bonds aren't strong enough for me to read your thoughts or feel your emotions yet. They will be eventually, hopefully, but until then you and I need to have an open book policy.

You can't assume I'll know or be able to figure everything out on my own. Otherwise we'll be right back where we started. So, what had you leaping off the couch like I bit you?"

Katrina studied him for a moment. His logic made sense. Much as she didn't want to admit it, if she kept the information to herself, he might assume she'd changed her mind about being with him, and that was the last thing she wanted. It was better to tell him the truth, embarrassing as it might be, rather than make things more difficult than they already were. How many years had she fought how she felt just to end up right where she would've been if she'd only been honest to begin with? There was no avoiding it. They belonged together. It was a scientific fact, as well as destiny. She could spend more useless time fighting it, making them both miserable, or she could swallow her pride and tell him everything.

"Am I the only one who must confess my feelings, or does this go both ways?"

"There will be no secrets between us."

Katrina nodded and focused on the ceiling above them rather than his expectant expression. "I was waiting for you to wake up because I have to pee, but I didn't want to wake you up because you looked so peaceful. I was studying you, and I decided our future children should have your eyelashes." She felt her cheeks burning, and she inhaled a deep breath in a useless attempt to calm herself.

Seth chuckled. "How long have you been waiting to go to the bathroom?"

She cleared her throat. "That's not the point."

"I know, Katrina." He kissed her forehead gently.

"Down that hall, first door on the right. The one on the left is a coat closet."

Katrina bolted up off the couch as if the thing was on fire and sprinted down the hall with Seth's laughter echoing after her. She scowled at herself in the mirror as she shoved the bathroom door closed behind her. She felt like an idiot. Surely this couldn't have been what he meant. She would've like to hide in the bathroom indefinitely, but short of climbing out the window and running home, there wasn't much Katrina could do but face him.

With her head held low in mortification, she finished up, washed her hands, and left the bathroom.

"Now, what were you saying about our future children," persisted Seth. He sat backward on the couch, his chin resting on the back of the cushion, staring at her like a kid on Christmas morning impatiently waiting for his first present. His big, round golden gaze was bright with interest, and he watched her inch around the room as she struggled to gather what remained of her pride.

"It was just a thought," mumbled Katrina shyly. "I wasn't implying—"

"Please, imply!" He grinned mischievously. "I desperately want to explore this topic with you."

Katrina cleared her throat nervously. "I wasn't exactly planning anything. I was just struck with how...attractive you are and thought I'd prefer if we ever did have children, that they look more like you." She didn't try to meet his gaze as she spoke.

"Really?" He pursed his lips thoughtfully. "I would prefer they look more like you. You have the most beautiful green eyes I've ever seen, even when they're scowling at me."

She could feel her cheeks burning once more, and her gaze darted around the room in an effort to keep from focusing on him. "I thought maybe I could talk Dezra into helping me find an apartment today…do you want to come too?"

"I have a better idea."

Her gaze met his, and he hopped over the back of the couch and took a few cautious steps toward her. "You could just move in here. With me."

Her heart pounded. "Now? Today?" She stared at him in wide-eyed shock. "Like right now?"

Seth nodded. "Whenever you want. There is plenty of space, and it's going to happen eventually, anyway. I don't see why it can't be now. Unless you don't want to? Do you need more time? I understand if—"

"If I say yes, it doesn't mean I'm going to have sex with you."

He grinned, the corner of his lip lifting confidently. "You do what you are comfortable with, whenever you feel like it. I'm not in any hurry. But my bed is super comfy if you want to share it—no sex. Just sleep."

Katrina inhaled a deep breath. "Yeah…ok." She glanced around the room once more, this time in a critical light rather than to avoid his gaze. "But if I change my mind about the sex part…"

His gaze swept over her, and she felt her body burn under his intense focus. "You do what you are comfortable with, whenever you feel like it. I'm not in any hurry." He repeated his earlier statement word for word.

Katrina felt at ease by his response. The repetition of his statement was enough to calm her raging fears.

"It's just that I've never had sex with anyone before, and I just want it to happen naturally. I don't want it to be a big deal or have to worry about whenever it does happen. Does that make sense?" She knew she was using her most clinical tone to voice her concerns, but it was the only way she could address her fears without feeling like she would prefer to melt into the floor or die of mortification. As a nearly thirty-year-old adult, she knew sex was something she should've experienced by now, but knowing she had a mate had made it seem pointless and wrong to be with anyone but him. And since she'd had no intention of seeing him, she'd just assumed to forget about it all together. She knew perfectly well how to relieve stress on her own without a partner, and while she'd been lonely, logically she understood that sex was not love, and that merely interacting with another person in that way would not make her any less lonely. In fact, she was sure she would regret it. Now that they were giving this mating thing a shot, however, it was a whole new ball game for her.

His head tilted curiously. "Perfectly."

"It does?" She stared at him in surprise. "You understand?"

"Absolutely. I only wish I could offer you the same innocence. I can assure you I only ever slept with a human, and I instantly regretted it. I decided after the one and only time that it would be you or no one. I hope you aren't disappointed...I thought you weren't interested." He looked sheepish, and Katrina absolutely refused to admit that there was an ounce of jealousy simmering not only in her cat, but herself as well. Seth was theirs, and no one else but them would touch him ever again if she had anything to say about it.

"What am I supposed to say exactly?" she asked carefully, unsure how to proceed.

He shrugged. "Whatever you want. But anything is preferable to nothing."

Katrina swallowed. "The truth?"

Seth nodded.

She struggled to process the range of emotions racing through her mind. She wasn't mad at him. That would've been ridiculous. She wasn't even mad at the human. That too was insane. She stared at him, unsure, and realized it wasn't technically jealousy either. The human side of her rationalized that everything he'd said was perfectly normal, but the cat in her was not pleased.

"I'm of two minds."

"Ok..." His nervous response made her heart hitch anxiously.

"The human in me accepts this as a natural biological development and realizes there is nothing to be concerned about. The cat in me is not quite so understanding."

He nodded. "And how does your cat feel?"

"She thinks I should claim you so we are the last one. She is possessive of you and would prefer I mark you once and for all. My cat is not quite as logical when it comes to you, and she affects my ability to reason."

Seth grinned triumphantly. "Your cat has nothing to worry about. I belong to you in every way."

Katrina shivered as a wave of heat washed over her, drenching her in relief and excitement. She wouldn't have thought something so simple could have such a big impact on her, but she could feel the fire burning at her core, fueled by his lazy mischievous grin.

She understood that her body's response was a natural reaction to desire, but there was nothing simple about her desire. She wasn't merely a human woman craving his attention. She was his mate, and her entire existence ached to have him close. Suddenly all the cliché romantic scenes in movies made absolute sense, and all those teenage fantasies about *dying if he never kissed her* were more realistic than the mature part of her brain that insisted it was only sex, nothing more.

If her cat could smirk, Katrina knew the lioness would be gloating. Her cat had tried for years to convince her they needed him, and Katrina had forced those predispositions to the back of her mind, insisting that her beast only understood animal instincts and didn't understand that they too were human and couldn't simply demand his attention as the mountain lion would have had they been wild animals.

"You seem pensive...Is she not content with my vow?"

She lifted her gaze toward Seth's. "My cat and I do not see eye to eye. Especially when it concerns you. I often fight her for control when you are close, which is another reason I try to avoid you." Katrina sighed.

"I learned incredibly early as a child that the only way to keep myself under control was to analyze my feelings as if they were facts rather than emotions. We are taught to keep ourselves hidden from humans and to keep our animal under control so we're not discovered, but I had such a hard time with my emotions. I felt everything so deeply that I had to leash my cat and sometimes disassociate from her—in order to keep her from becoming too much for me to handle. The more I tried to control her, the more feral she became. I struggled every day to ignore what she wanted..."

Katrina frowned in frustration. "It's so hard to explain...it was just easier for me to stay away from you, but she did not agree with that choice."

"She doesn't let you hide from your emotions." Seth nodded understandingly. "Logically you realize that isn't healthy for either of you...right?"

Katrina huffed. "If I don't, I'm an emotional wreck."

"Then be a wreck—with me, Kat. You can be yourself. I accept you exactly as you are."

Katrina winced. Seth was the only one she'd ever allowed to use that nickname, but he was also the only one she'd ever hidden from. "You don't know what you're asking."

"Yes, I do. We all go through the same thing, but most of us don't shut down our emotions. The rest of us are raging, hot-blooded animals who are quick to react and easy to anger. Shifters are naturally more dangerous than the rest of the other kin races. We're aware of this, and we are careful, but when in the presence of our own, we don't hide who we are. You are the only shifter I know who is just as controlled at home as you are in public."

"That's why your friends call me an ice princess," agreed Katrina softly, recalling how hurt she'd been the first time she'd heard them hiss the word from behind their hands. They didn't think she would hear them, but Katrina's cat had picked up on their taunt as easily as if they'd said it to her face. She smiled sadly. "It wasn't my intention to be cold. It was just the only way I knew how to stay in control. An icy exterior is an excellent shield when you're emotionally unstable... When you first came to the pride, and all the kids had to meet with your father as the pride's new beta. He doled out advice for each one of us according to how we responded. I wasn't as robotic as I am now." She smiled, remembering that day as clearly as she did when she first met Seth himself. "My mother used to call me her little hellcat. I was practically wild. But I was a danger to our hard-fought secrecy, and he told me I needed to protect my family by imagining my cat in a cage so that I could learn how to control myself better. I realize he didn't mean it the way I applied it to my life, but the idea that I could expose us was terrifying, and I decided that I would never let myself be free like that again. It was too dangerous."

Seth scowled. "He teaches all the young shifters that lesson, but you're the first who's ever taken his advice literally. The rest of us shrug it off and go on making mistakes."

"Dezra did the same. I envied her that freedom. I wanted to be more like her, but it seemed too much of a risk. My family was safer this way." Katrina shrugged. "I did realize my mistake later on, but at this point it's easier to admit I don't have as many feelings."

"Easier—not better. You can't do this your whole life, Kat. What if we do have kids? Would you have them think you don't love them?"

Katrina had never considered how her emotionless responses might look to someone else, but when put into perspective, she imagined how she'd feel if her own parents treated her the way she'd treated so many others, and her heart hurt. Tears filled her eyes, and she swiped them away immediately, as if ashamed they'd ever existed.

"I'm starting to think you need me as much as I need you. Honestly, I thought I was the only desperate one here. You have to trust me to help you, Kat. I can handle whatever you can dish out. I swear."

****

Seth watched his mate struggle and felt his own heart hammering inside his chest. Katrina was miserable. He could see it as clearly as he could the early morning sun streaming through his living room window. He wasn't sure how he'd missed it before. Maybe she was that good at hiding it, or maybe he'd been too focused on his own misery to see it, but now that he understood, there was no way he wasn't going to help her.

Every instinct in Seth's entire body was screaming at him to push her. Even his cat wanted to taunt her until she released all the pent-up emotions she'd been hoarding away. She couldn't physically hurt him, but he'd take every oral insult she could think to hurl at him if it meant relieving her of even a fraction of the fear he saw lingering in her eyes every time he asked for the truth. Katrina had said she wasn't afraid of him. She was afraid of how he made her feel, and oh how he wanted to make her feel!

"Kat?"

She stared at him, her mouth set in a grim line. "Yes?" Her response was automatic, and suddenly all the years he'd spent trying to get her attention made perfect sense. Any other teenage girl would've seen his awkward flirting for what it was or at least have gotten pissed off enough to confront him. But his Kat hadn't understood. He still didn't think she did.

"You're not cold. I'm sorry they said that. It must've hurt."

Katrina lifted her chin defensively. "It can only hurt if I let it."

Seth snorted. "That's a lie, and you know it. They hurt you. Admit it. You wanted to fit in like everyone else. You wanted to respond to me. You wanted just as much as the rest of us, but you didn't let yourself."

Her bottom lip quivered, but her gaze remained unmoved.

"You can't hurt me, Kat."

This time she clenched her jaw.

"Tell me about your cat," demanded Seth, trying a different tactic. If she couldn't be poked, maybe he could convince her to let her guard down.

"What about her? She isn't much different than yours."

"Somehow I highly doubt that. Unlike you, I have a tendency to listen to my beast. What does she want you to do right now?"

Katrina's neon green gaze brightened with interest. "She wants to bite you."

Seth purred in satisfaction. He couldn't help it—the sound was out before he could stop himself. The idea of her perfectly pointed pearly fangs descending from her gums and biting into his flesh had every part of him at attention.

"And why would she want to do that?" he asked, knowing perfectly well why. Seth's own cat had voiced as much for years.

"Her opinion or mine?"

"Strictly hers."

Katrina swallowed. "No one else can have you if

we mark you."

Seth barely contained the urge to rub his face against hers like a damned house cat demanding attention. He'd longed to hear her say such things for so many years, and now that she was saying them it took every bit of willpower he had not to react accordingly.

"Why would she care if anyone else wanted me?" It was a dumb question. Shifters were notoriously possessive, but maybe if he got her talking from her cat's point of view the beast would force her to release some of her bottled-up emotions.

"Because you are ours." Her eyes widened. "I mean—hers."

Seth shrugged as if she hadn't exposed a tiny bit of her feelings just then. He didn't want her shutting down. "How does your cat feel about me having slept with someone else?"

Her eyes flashed, and Seth knew he'd hit a soft spot. He prepared himself for her wrath, hoping it wouldn't be too brutal.

"She is pissed." Katrina shrugged nonchalantly, and Seth was almost disappointed that the fire in her eyes did not leak from her lips.

"That's all?"

Kat inched toward one of the bar stools sitting next to the kitchen counter by the couch and sank carefully onto the surface. Her hands gripped the seat under her, and he saw her knuckles paling in response. She wasn't nearly as untouched as she was trying to pretend to be.

Seth grinned. "She's only pissed? Her mate had the audacity to seek attention from someone who wasn't her, and she's just mad?" He hummed. "I guess it's not that big of a deal…"

Katrina chuckled, but there was a touch of sarcasm in her tone. "No big deal."

"She probably wouldn't care if I did it again, then?"

A feline snarl slipped from her lips, and Seth nearly grinned. There wasn't a prayer in hell of him ever touching anyone but her, and he'd already told her so, but in the heat of the moment her cat wasn't thinking straight. The beast didn't think human thoughts. She only knew how to react to things directly in front of her, like Seth considering another woman. Seth knew that, because like her, his cat was much the same. It was often hard to separate the two, but Kat seemed to have made a career out of doing so. "She would appreciate it if you kept your hands off of others from now on," admitted Kat, her words barely audible through her clenched teeth.

"It's the scent thing, right? Smelling another on me?"

Kat closed her eyes, and Seth could practically feel the fury she was trying so hard to contain.

"A human scent washes off easily enough though, right? If I was discreet?"

Kat hissed, and her eyes popped open. She was no longer hiding the anger in her gaze as she hopped off the stool and closed the distance between them.

Seth could hardly breathe as he watched her stalk closer and closer until she was just beneath his nose, filling his senses with her delicious scent. She reached up and snatched the front of his shirt, balling it in her fist as she scowled up at him. It was the most adorable thing he'd ever seen; he knew she wasn't nearly as angry as she could've been if he did cheat on her—

which he *never* would, but that didn't seem to matter to her cat.

"You are my mate; it is too *late* for you to choose another."

Not *our mate* noted Seth triumphantly. Hers. She'd said he was her mate. His cat purred, but Seth wisely managed to keep the sound from escaping his lips. "Mhm." He agreed with a soft hum, but she didn't seem to catch his response.

Kat's grip tightened. "I've tortured myself over you for years, and I am not going to let you go now."

Seth tried to stop himself, but hearing her proclaim how much she'd wanted him was more than he could handle. He wrapped his fingers around her wrist and pulled her closer. Kat was still scowling at him when he pressed his mouth against hers. He tugged his shirt from her hand and wound her arm around his back to settle on his hips. Her fist opened as he released her, and she pulled him closer, forcing her body against his as if she couldn't get close enough.

He wasn't complaining. He fisted his hand in her hair and dragged her mouth against his, desperate to taste her. She was like cinnamon and honey, sweet but spicy, enticing him. Her scent called to him like a siren's song, demanding his attention, and he gave in to her without hesitation. His gums throbbed, and his fangs ached to descend and sink into her soft flesh. He wanted so badly to bind her to him, but he knew he shouldn't. Not when she was hurting. Kisses were one thing, but their mating would not be forged in anger.

Chapter Four

Lyndra Osyn knew it was wrong. She stared at the computer screen, her fingers tapping nervously against the edge of her mouse as she contemplated what she was about to do. She didn't want to, but she had no choice.

She considered the money and what she'd do with it when it arrived safely in her account. Not technically her account, but an account she had access to. One she could safely transport another ten thousand into.

A woman down the hall screamed as her husband put his fist through the wall, and Lyndra flinched. She'd lived here most of her life, and she should've been used to the sounds by now, but she hated the violence. In the other room, she heard moaning, and inhaled a deep breath. She had to do it again. She had no choice.

Lyndra returned her attention to the computer screen once more. There was so much money in their account. She knew they wouldn't miss a small amount. If they had, they would have come after her by now. They had plenty, she reminded herself as she began typing, forcing her fingers to fly over the keyboard.

The account holder was a cat. That much she knew. Therefore, the passcode would be some complicated arrangement of numbers and letters that would only make sense to a select few. Lyndra didn't have much time to figure it out, however. She only hoped she could get through the firewall before the network alerted the account holder to her presence. It was worth it to get caught she decided as tears streaked down her cheeks. Ten thousand dollars was enough. It had to be. She couldn't keep taking from the cat. It wasn't right.

She'd been trying for hours to get through, and all she'd learned was that the woman's name was Katrina Valenthia and that she was a cat. She was also from the city, just like Lyndra, which made Katrina more dangerous because she was close enough to retaliate if she discovered Lyndra had been the one to take her money. Lyndra knew from experience what an angry shifter could do, especially a rogue, but she knew she was running out of options. There were worse things than shifters, at least as far as she was concerned.

Lyndra stared at the screen through the tears in her eyes, but she didn't bother to wipe them away. There wasn't enough time. Within minutes she discovered other names on the account—a Ward Valenthia, Sammara Valenthia, Dezra Valenthia, Varg Mourgent, and finally a Seth Mourgent. All of them had access to this account, which meant all of them could see what she had done. Lyndra was fairly certain all of them were cats too, which meant she'd have a small pride out looking for her if she was caught. Fresh tears rolled down her face, and she sniffed as snot puddled beneath her nose. *She couldn't get caught. She wouldn't.*

It didn't matter how wrong she felt for taking their money. They didn't need all of it. It wasn't fair that they had so much! She just needed a little more. Only a little. The firewall beeped, signaling she'd finally cracked the code, and Lyndra stared at the numbers on the account listing how much money was available and free for the taking. It had taken her so much longer this time. Surely the cats had seen what she'd done...

Just ten thousand. They wouldn't miss that small amount. Lyndra tried to convince herself that what she was doing was okay, but in her heart she knew it wasn't. It was so wrong.

****

Katrina wasn't sure what happened. One minute she was safely perched on the edge of Seth's barstool, slamming her cat into the kennel she'd erected for the mouthy beast, and the next she was in his arms, purring. He was kissing her, and he felt so good against her body. He tasted like perfection, and every bit of her wanted more. The cat was loose, and every emotion Katrina couldn't hide was pouring from her in titanic waves, rushing at him in an uncontrollable tsunami of lust, relief, and...love?

She balked and slammed a lid on the emotions she felt rushing through her. She knew he wasn't unaffected. Even without mature mating bonds to tell him, there was absolutely no way Seth hadn't felt what she had forced on him. Katrina ripped herself from his arms and stumbled backward a few steps, her eyes wild with terror.

He stared at her, and his pupils—usually human— had gone feline. His fangs had descended, and he was panting as if he'd run a mile. He didn't say a word, but his gaze was wide and just as untamed as she felt. The scent of his desire rolled off him, drowning her in the urge to rub her body against his, and she hissed in response.

"Kat..."

She shook her head and leapt past him toward the

front door. Seth didn't chase her—not immediately. He must've given her plenty of a head start, because before she knew it, Katrina had willed her clothes into the nether between worlds and was running naked in her feline form, covered from head to toe in sandy blonde fur, her whiskers pressed back against her cheeks, her tail out behind her, giving her perfect balance as she ran with all the power she could muster. Away from the houses where her pride lived and up into the forest behind them where her father owned several hundred acres, and she could run freely into the mountains, away from Seth and all the emotions he invoked.

Katrina ran until her calves burned and her lungs begged for relief, until with a groan of misery she collapsed in a heap and simply felt everything her mate had forced to the surface of her soul—everything she'd been burying for so long.

A familiar scent, far less enticing than it had been hours earlier drifted in on a slight breeze, but she didn't even bother to lift her head. She lay in the fresh cool grass, letting her own emotions wash over her, simply feeling the world spin beneath her.

Katrina heard the soft wisps of his feather-light paws as he made his way through the grass toward her, and though her ears flicked in his direction, she did not move. Her body felt too heavy, weighted by all the feelings she'd repressed over the years.

His nose brushed against her ribs, then her shoulder, and eventually her jaw, before he collapsed next to her much more gracefully. He lay next to her, as regal as any mountain lion she'd ever seen, his head raised and alert for danger while Katrina felt like she might actually die. He didn't shift or try to talk to her.

He didn't offer comfort, but he sat in silence, watching over her.

Seth. Her mate. The kid who'd smiled that goofy toothy grin, who'd offered her a bit of his lunch when she'd forgotten hers. He'd been so kind to her in the beginning, but she'd been too afraid to be his friend because that would've meant unleashing emotions, and she couldn't do that. She'd pretended to ignore his efforts, but the sweet boy who'd offered her his tuna sandwich was the same guy who sat next to her now, guarding her. Her heart broke for the way he must've felt. She was his mate, and she'd treated him as if he meant nothing to her.

Katrina lifted her head and was about to shift back into her human self when the decaying scent of a rogue shifter interrupted her train of thought.

Seth was on his feet in an instant. His fur stood on end, and he stepped over her, protecting her from the rogue that had just appeared past the tree line.

The creature was feline, like them, but he was no longer human. His beast had been eaten by the dark residue of magic and turned into the monster they saw now, a cougar with fur stained by blood and eyes as red as the setting sun.

Seth snarled a warning, but the rogue didn't even hesitate. He moved toward them like a predator with prey in his sights.

Katrina was absolutely terrified. She wasn't trained. She'd never been so close to a rogue in her entire life! She knew almost nothing about defending herself, let alone her mate, against this particular kind of threat. Luckily, Seth knew exactly what he was doing and would no doubt have handled the rogue in spectacular runner fashion, if there hadn't been a second one.

Katrina rose to her feet. She was exhausted, but her cat ignored those pains and focused on the new threat. Not a cougar like the other, but still feline and just as dangerous. The second rogue, a jaguar, stalked toward her from the other side of the tree line, taking advantage of a distracted Seth, who was valiantly defending Katrina against the rogue cougar.

The rogue jaguar snarled, and his fangs were yellowed with rot. His breath was as putrid as his scent, and he was easy enough to avoid as he moved in for the kill.

Evasive maneuvers were about the only thing Katrina had learned throughout her years in school, and only because she secretly liked to watch Seth train after classes. She'd sat in the trees and watched him practice with the other runners, and she'd ached to cheer him on, but that cool collected human in her had forced her to keep her distance. She regretted that now, but she was glad she'd at least learned something from him.

The rogue cougar pinned Seth momentarily, and Katrina felt her heart sink to the soles of her paws. He was in trouble. She ducked to avoid the lunging jaguar once more and made a beeline for her mate, but Seth was already back on his feet. By the time she was within mere feet of him, he'd pinned the cougar, but they were still battling for dominance, a fight Katrina knew Seth would win, if there wasn't another rogue ready and waiting to attack the instant he turned his back.

Katrina knew she should be doing more than avoiding the jaguar's attacks, but she hoped if she kept the second rogue busy long enough, and maybe tired the monster out, Seth would have no problem dispatching them.

Too late, Katrina realized she'd led the second rogue right to her mate, and the jaguar was already preparing to pounce, his powerful shoulders rotating over and over.

She needed to make herself a better target, she decided as she ran at the rogue to get its attention. The jaguar took the bait, and Katrina shifted back into her human self, completely clothed, and looking for all the world like a vulnerable human ripe for the killing. "Here, kitty, kitty," called Katrina breathlessly. "Come on, kitty, kitty, this way." She danced on the tips of her toes, ready to duck and roll when the jaguar lunged.

The jaguar stalked toward her just as the first rogue yelped in pain. All eyes were on Seth as he ended the first rogue's life. But Katrina didn't have time to cheer. The second rogue was already sprinting toward her mate once more.

Her pulse raced as she ran after the rogue, not nearly as fast in her human form with sensitive human feet on rocky, uneven terrain. He would reach Seth before she could.

Seth snarled as the rogue leapt and landed on his back. The rogue's teeth sank deep into his fur, and the scent of fresh blood blinded Katrina to anything but his pain. She had to help him before it was too late! New tears flooded her gaze as she rushed toward the snarling cats, but these were for Seth, the man who'd waited so long for her to come to her senses.

The jaguar ripped through Seth's shoulder, and Seth yelped in much the same way the first rogue had.

The rogue rolled away from the male mountain lion and stalked him as Seth stumbled. He tried to get up, but whatever the jaguar had done had caused too much damage, and Katrina recognized a death pounce when she saw one. If Seth had been with his team this wouldn't have happened. Instead he'd followed Katrina as she'd run blindly into the mountains, uncaring for her own safety—or his—and been left to defend her against not one, but two rogues.

Good thing he'd killed the first rogue, or Katrina wouldn't stand a chance as she shifted once more and launched herself at the jaguar.

Momentarily stunned by her bravado, the jaguar hesitated, then clearly seeing her as a bigger threat, he started toward her instead.

"Katrina, no!" Seth was human again, and his shoulder was pouring blood from two gigantic feline bite marks that punctured his shoulder blade. She noticed yet more injuries to his calf where the first rogue had attacked and knew he wouldn't be able to walk, let alone go after the jaguar.

Katrina considered luring the jaguar back to her pride and letting them handle the rogue, but every instinct in her refused to leave Seth unguarded in the mountains. She considered her options and circled back toward the other feline. He was injured too, she realized, but not nearly as badly as Seth seemed to be. The rogue limped, and Katrina saw the opportunity as it presented itself.

"Katrina, stop!" Seth's panicked voice got the rogue's attention once more, and the jaguar spun and zipped back up the mountain toward him.

Katrina cursed and hurried after the beast, using

every bit of her speed to catch up to him and knock him off his feet once more.

The jaguar was furious now as he got back up and shook himself off. Evidently Seth was no longer a threat, and the rogue now stalked toward Katrina with a glint in his blood-red gaze. His intention deadly clear.

Her pulse ripped through her veins. She'd saved Seth but at the cost of her own safety. She couldn't defend her mate, and she sure as hell couldn't defend herself. All she knew about being a rogue hunter was from spying on Seth, and she'd never once tried any of the moves out, but they were as ingrained in her head as his scent, and she had no choice but to attempt one of the many maneuvers she'd watched him perfect on the field.

Katrina remembered thinking Seth moved with all the power and grace of his cat, and despite being the exact same species as him she knew her body would not twist as beautifully as his could. She'd be a flip-flopping mess, and a disgrace to her race, but she had no choice. She'd happily embarrass herself in front of her mate if it meant saving his life. She doubted her skills, but his sweat-slicked, glistening body appeared in her mind, and she mimicked the powerful twist she'd seem him accomplish at only sixteen. Then, as the rogue lunged past her, caught off guard by her mid-air rotation, she launched herself back into the air and spun, landing almost perfectly on the rogue's back.

The rogue shifted his weight, and she nearly lost her grip, but she held on long enough to sink her fangs into the beast's collar bone. It snarled and clawed at her, but Katrina rolled away from his powerful claws, her feline jaws still locked on his throat. A sick sucking sound put a stop to the cat's thrashing, and blood gushed across her neck and chest.

Katrina had no idea what happened. Her eyes were closed, and she was holding on for dear life, flopping around like a fish out of water, and then all of a sudden there was no resistance, and the jaguar was bleeding profusely on the ground. Dead.

She shifted back into her human self and backed away on her hands and feet from the dead cat. "Holy shit!" She spit a mouthful of the jaguar's blood and fur from her mouth and stared in shock at the dead rogue. "I killed him! Oh Hades…I killed him!" Tears sprang to her eyes as she spun and ran back up the mountain, half crawling as she made her way to Seth's side.

He was sitting up against a tree, his shoulder still glistening with fresh blood, and he was panting. Tears were sliding down his cheeks, and Katrina knew he must've been in a lot of pain, but Seth was shaking his head, and he reached out with his uninjured arm to pull her close.

"My beautiful Kat, you scared the fuck out of me!" He sobbed as he held her against his chest. "I can't believe you—you did a perfect spiral!" His sobs of relief turned to ones of happiness. "You kicked his ass!" He grinned through his tears and showered her face in proud kisses. "My Kat."

Katrina hardly dared to breathe as Seth clutched her shaking body to his. "We need to get back home before any others get any stupid ideas," he muttered.

She nodded agreeably, unable to voice a proper response. She'd been so sure she was going to die, and then she'd taken that man's life…it had been too easy. Her fangs had ripped through his throat, and she'd felt the life drain from his body. Katrina's soul ached, but Seth was alive, and that was all that mattered in that moment.

"My beautiful, perfect Kat. You're so amazing," whispered Seth as he limped down the mountainside, with her supporting his weight beneath his uninjured shoulder. "Where did you learn that?" he demanded breathlessly as he pressed another series of kisses against her temple.

"From you," she admitted reluctantly.

He chuckled. "When?"

"In high school. I used to sit in the apple trees outside the field and watch you practice. I'm so sorry. I shouldn't have spied on you, but..."

"But what," teased Seth, his lips still lingering near her forehead.

"You're so pretty," groaned Katrina. "It isn't fair!"

Seth laughed out loud. "Pretty?"

"The way your body moves and your skin glows." Katrina groaned. "I couldn't help it. The cat in me had to see you, even if the human in me refused to get any closer. I couldn't resist watching you. The way you perfected every skill was so hypnotic. I couldn't think straight!"

"You used those apple trees to hide your scent. I would've known you were there otherwise," he accused playfully. "I would've showed off if I'd known you were watching."

"You weren't showing off?" Katrina swallowed.

"I was trying to be good enough for you."

Katrina sobbed. "I'm emotionally stunted, Seth. Why the hell would you think you're the one who isn't good enough? I'm the messed-up one!"

Seth chuckled. "Not anymore."

He was right. From the moment he'd kissed her that morning, something inside of her had broken open and released a dam of feelings all over him, but he was still standing. She'd ran from him and emptied herself in the grass, and he would've been just fine if those damned rogues hadn't shown up. She searched herself and found her cat purring. The imaginary cage Katrina had erected was gone, and for the first time since she was a child, they were one again.

"You fixed me." Katrina's voice was barely a hiss. She doubted he'd even be able to hear her, but his grip tightened in response.

"You weren't broken, Kat. I only showed you what you were already capable of."

She sobbed once more, this time in relief.

****

Katrina was bawling into his shoulder, and the rogue's blood was mixing with her tears, but if anyone had an idea to attack her just then, her appearance would scare even the most seasoned hunters. She looked like a gods-be-damned-warrior and aced the part, absolutely, stunning. If he wasn't already in pain trying his hardest just to breathe, she would've robbed him of every bit of oxygen in his body.

His Katrina had saved his life—using moves she'd learned from him! She'd spied on him! He wanted so badly to laugh, but he was pretty damn sure the rogue had broken a few ribs and that one of them might've punctured his lung. It wasn't a death sentence by any means, but it would prohibit him from making love to her the way he wanted to so badly, at least for a few days.

He let her lead him back down the mountain, his body on fire with each step. Seth would've preferred to collapse and lie there until one of his teammates discovered him, but he didn't dare keep Katrina exposed to rogues any longer than he already had. He should've tried to stop her, but he knew she'd needed the run as much as he had. Her scent had been driving him crazy for years, and now she was finally within reach, and he'd nearly lost every bit of self-control he possessed.

They reached the bottom of the mountain in twice the amount of time it had taken them to climb it, and within seconds, his pride mates were swarming them, demanding to know what had happened. Two of his teammates joined the group. Brothers, Lennix and Luc, helped Kat half carry him as he struggled to breathe, and his mind began to swim with relief. His Kat was safe now.

Chapter Five

Katrina didn't have much choice but to allow the two male felines to take over when Seth passed out. She followed them like a stray cat as they made their way to his home. One of the brothers ordered the curious pride members who trailed behind them to Seth's house to remain outside and wait for their alpha. Then the four of them made their way into the split level. They continued up the stairs and into the bedroom, which she'd never seen. They carefully laid Seth on the bed and began stripping him out of his bloody clothes.

She should've left then. She wasn't much use to Luc or Lennix, but neither of them said anything about her leaving, and so she remained. Quietly waiting by the door in case they needed her to do something to help with Seth.

"What the hell happened," demanded the one she knew to be Luc.

Katrina debated on what to tell them. A half-truth or all of what happened. They wouldn't confront her, if not out of respect for Seth but for her dad their alpha, but Seth had given her a gift more precious than anything she'd ever been given, and his friends deserved to know everything.

"He followed me into the mountain," admitted Katrina.

"Of course he did. He'd follow you through the

fires of hell. But why," growled Luc.

"Because I ran from him."

"Because she's the ice princess. Why else would she run from Seth?" huffed Lennix .

Katrina flinched. These two had been among those who'd began the infamous nickname she'd grown up despising.

"You know Seth hates when you call her that," muttered Luc.

Typically, Katrina would've buried her feelings on the matter in the deepest pits of her gut and kept on repressing her emotions, but Seth had set her free, and there were many pros to his gift, but there were also cons, and apparently this was one of them. Tears immediately sprang to her eyes as old hurt came rushing back, and she swallowed the urge to cry.

It wasn't just the nickname. She'd heard it often enough that even if she hadn't lost the ability to express her emotions accurately, she still should have been used to it, but combined with her feelings of guilt for having gotten Seth hurt in the first place, she lost the will to put on the old unfeeling mask she'd donned so well.

When she didn't respond, Luc glanced back at her and immediately cursed. "Seth is going to murder you, Lennix," he muttered.

"What, why?" demanded Lennix. He too glanced back at her and groaned. "Shit, Katrina, I didn't mean it. Please don't cry! Seth will never forgive me!"

Katrina shook her head. She wanted to tell them it wasn't their fault, but it partially was, and they'd know she was lying.

The front door of Seth's house opened and slammed shut, followed by the sound of two heavy adult males running up the stairs.

Katrina immediately moved out of the way as her father and Seth's burst into the room.

"What happened?" demanded Varg, Seth's father.

"Rogues I'm guessing. He sure smells like he's tangled with one or two," explained Luc, and he immediately moved out of the way for his alpha and the beta to examine Seth.

"Who was with him? Why was he in the mountains alone?" growled Katrina's father.

Luc and Lennix glanced at one another.

"He wasn't alone," mumbled Katrina tearfully.

"Katrina?" Her father spun as if he hadn't realized she was there. "You're covered in blood! Are you hurt too? What the hell happened?"

Katrina inhaled a deep breath. "Seth was trying to help me…I went up the mountain, and he followed me. Two rogues jumped him."

"Hell! Are they alive? Somebody needs to go after them," exclaimed her father.

"They're dead," admitted Katrina softly.

"He killed both of them?" asked Varg in surprise.

Katrina shook her head. "No. He killed the first one."

"Then who—" Her father hesitated. "You?"

"I defended him."

"You could have been killed," gasped Varg in shock. "You're not trained!"

"It was me or Seth, and I wasn't just going to leave him defenseless against the rogue! He was hurt!" Katrina scowled at the four men staring at her.

"But…how?" gasped her father.

"It's complicated." Katrina lifted her chin, ignoring

the tears that still trickled down her cheeks. "Will he be all right?"

Her father nodded. "He will be fine. He just needs to sleep and heal. I'm sure he's in good hands now." Katrina's father glanced between Luc, Lennix, and Katrina. "I'll have someone drop your suitcase off. I'm sure you'll want to watch over him while he recovers."

Katrina nodded wordlessly, and her father breezed out of the room as quickly as he'd arrived.

"I know my son appreciates you being here, Katrina." Varg patted her on the back and followed the same path her father had taken, leaving her with Luc and Lennix.

"Did I miss something?" growled Lennix, his eyes wide as he stared at Katrina. "Since when do you cry over something we say? I thought you were above us thickheaded runners."

"Leave her alone, or Seth really will kick your ass," warned Luc.

"I didn't hurt him on purpose," muttered Katrina. Once upon a time she'd have never justified her actions to people like the two standing before her. She wouldn't have cared enough to defend herself. But these were Seth's friends. They cared about Seth too. She couldn't just ignore them and pretend their words meant nothing to her anymore. Not if she wanted to have a good relationship with her mate.

"You ignored him," growled Lennix.

"I'm serious, Lennix," snapped Luc. "You can't pick on her. You know how he gets!"

"She's been treating our best friend like he doesn't matter since the day we met her. Let Seth be pissed. She deserves to know what she did." Lennix crossed his arms angrily.

Katrina didn't blame the brothers one bit. Lennix was right, and even if it had been unintentional, she hurt Seth. "I wasn't always like this. I was told that I had to confine myself in order to protect the pride, and I thought that meant I had to stop expressing how I felt. I shut my cat away in order to control myself. I knew Seth was my mate, but that was it! I didn't realize he liked me. I thought he was teasing me to get a laugh out of his friends. I thought he was picking on me! I couldn't even process my own emotions, and logically there was no reason someone like Seth would want a girl like me."

The brothers glanced at one another in confusion.

"A girl like you?" asked Luc, finally speaking up on Seth's behalf.

"Seth is…" Katrina hesitated. "He's amazing. He has friends who love him, he's smart, talented, and strong. He's patient and considerate, and he could've had any girl he wanted. I was none of those things. I was so in my own head. He deserved a mate who was pretty and kind and who could get along with his friends. I'm not that girl. I tried to tell him that, but he doesn't listen."

"That's because he's in love with you, princess, and he has been since he was fifteen, but I doubt even he realized that," said Luc kindly, as if he understood where she was coming from.

"He won't even go to Nia's after work because of you," muttered Lennix with a nod. "I'd say he's got to be in love with you to ignore those hungry females."

"Besides, maybe you don't realize it, but you're not exactly ugly, Katrina. As far as felines go, you're definitely in the top five." Luc shrugged. "But if you tell Seth I said that he'll kill me. He has a soft spot when it comes to you."

"Shit, if I hadn't thought you were such a bitch, I would've considered you hot as hell." Lennix snorted. "Seth certainly could've done worse."

Katrina rolled her eyes. "Thanks?"

"The point is, we might've misjudged you, and we're sorry for that. We want Seth to be happy, and that means you, so if you're willing to forgive us for being assholes, then we'd like a do-over. We don't want to lose our friend over this." Luc stared at her hopefully. "What do you say, princess?"

"Why do you keep calling me princess?" asked Katrina with a suspicious scowl.

"Because you're the alpha's daughter. We call Dezra that too. She just doesn't get offended like you do," admitted Lennix .

"That's because you've never implied that she was heartless." Katrina raised one eyebrow in challenge, daring them to deny the truth.

"We said we were sorry," growled Lennix.

Katrina switched her gaze to Seth and sighed. He was naked and covered in only a sheet, but his skin was still stained with blood, both his and the rogue's. He was bruised and battered and clearly hurt more than he'd let on, but he'd risked his life for her, and if these two jerks were his friends, then she could manage to get along with them, maybe eventually even like them so long as they didn't taunt her anymore.

"All right, fine. For Seth."

****

Luc and Lennix managed to stick around for an

hour while Katrina showered and changed. She'd eventually convinced them to leave on the promise that she would call them when Seth finally woke up.

Alone with her mate, Katrina rummaged through his kitchen to find a washcloth and a large mixing bowl, which she filled with hot soapy water, then carted both back into his room and set the items on his bedside table. She needed to wash away the dried blood still littering Seth's beautiful flesh.

Her mouth watered at the sight of him, and her cat whined to curl up next to him, but the human in her merely kept washing. She pacified her cat with a vow to let Seth do whatever he wanted to them the instant he was well enough and went about finding a clean blanket to cover him with before she carted the rest of the bloody mess down to the laundry room to wash.

Moments later she'd retrieved her phone and was curled up in bed next to his uninjured side, comforted by the heat of his body near hers, scrolling through the digital rendition of her art gallery, checking to see if any paintings had recently sold and how much money she'd be able to contribute to the pride accounts when Seth finally began to stir.

"Son of a bitch," he groaned. "That bastard hit hard."

Katrina immediately recoiled away from him. "Am I hurting you?"

"No! Don't go." He inhaled a deep wheezing breath. "Stay. Please."

She settled into a sitting position next to him. "Damages?"

"Broken rib or two, probably a punctured lung, and a bruised shoulder bone…the rest are flesh wounds, I think. You?" His heated gaze raked over her body, and he grinned. "Pure perfection."

Katrina rolled her eyes. "I'm supposed to call your friends when you wake up."

"Pretend I'm not awake yet. I don't want those assholes ruining this moment."

"Those assholes love you, Seth."

"And I love you," admitted Seth softly.

Katrina inhaled a deep breath. "You do?"

"More than life itself, Kat."

Her heart thumped heavily, and she bit her lip anxiously. "I love you too."

He grinned. "Because I saved your life?"

"No, jerk, because I love you!" Katrina pouted prettily. "I'd have to be stupid not to."

"And you're definitely not stupid," chuckled Seth. He groaned then and clutched his side. "No laughing for a couple days."

"Exactly. Dad says you should be fine with some rest. So you just lie there and let me know if you need anything while I go hunt down your friends."

"Don't leave. My phone is on this table."

Katrina hopped off the bed and went around to the bedside stand to find a cell phone lying on top. It was fully charged, with a cord running from it through the back of the drawer, and she unplugged it, then held it out toward Seth to unlock.

"The passcode is the year we met."

"The year you joined our pride," declared Katrina. Her heart was doing all kinds of funny flips now, and there was nothing she could do to make them stop. Every word out of his mouth only reminded her how stupid she'd been to shut him out. She pressed in the numbers correlating with the year she'd met him, and the phone unlocked to show a picture of Seth, Luc, Lennix, and a couple others she knew but had never really talked to. The picture was blurry and focused on something—or rather someone behind them sitting alone at a picnic table, scowling at the pages of a math book. For a moment, Katrina was quiet. That girl had been so alone, and it showed, but the person who took the picture was alone too, even with all his friends around him. His friends were smiling, but his head was turned in her direction, and he looked just as sad as Katrina felt.

"I'll change it," whispered Seth knowingly.

Katrina swallowed. "I'll give you a better one." She smiled softly down at him, and he reached up attentively with his injured arm, and rested his hand on her hip, drawing her closer to the edge of the bed where he lay.

"I'm sorry," whispered Katrina with an aching heart. "I wish I could go back and undo it...I would do it so differently the second time."

"I would've tried harder." Seth smiled as he spoke. "We're here now though, and I'm not giving up on you."

She tried to convince herself not to cry again, but there were tears in her eyes as she scrolled through his contacts to find Luc's number. She hit the call button and turned on the speaker so Seth would be able to hear too.

"Seth?" Luc answered on the first ring.

"I'm alive," growled Seth with a grin.

"You damned well better be. How dare you let a couple of bastard rogues get the jump on you! I thought you were better than that!"

Seth shook his head, still grinning. "We're supposed to be on vacation. Apparently they didn't get the memo."

"We stopped by Nia's. She's making some kind of casserole thing for you so your mate doesn't have to cook while she's tending to your boo-boos. We'll bring it over in a little while. You need anything else?"

Katrina held her breath. She'd longed for friends like his, but she'd been too numb to let herself feel anything for anyone, and now it was too late.

"I'm fine. Thanks though."

She waited for Luc to say his goodbyes as well, then ended the call and went back around to the other side of the bed once more, where she scrolled through Seth's phone until she found the camera app. "Try not to look like you were nearly killed," she teased, as she flipped the phone camera around, leaned in close, and pressed her lips against his cheek. She checked the picture a moment later and was struck with just how much Seth must have meant it when he'd said he loved her. He didn't smile in the picture, but he looked at peace, and his eyes were closed as if a kiss on the cheek was the best thing that had ever happened to him. "How's that?" she whispered as she handed him his phone.

"Perfect." He grinned, and she retrieved her own phone as he fiddled with the wallpaper image.

Katrina had just put in her own passcode to unlock her phone when the notification light flashed at the top. Her pulse leapt, and she rushed to check the account transfer alert at the top of her screen. "Shit! I knew it would happen again!"

"The accounts?" asked Seth, as if he could read her mind.

"Yes, that asshole took another ten thousand! I didn't even have time to transfer the rest of the money like Dad wanted."

"And they still only took ten?" Seth frowned. "Weird."

"I know!" Katrina immediately began fiddling with the settings. Everything was exactly as she'd left it other than the firewall breach, which meant the hacker had figured out the password. Her heart slammed against her chest. "They guessed the password," she whispered in surprise. "Everyone on the account has their own personal password, and the thief guessed mine.

She scanned the transfers. "And I can't trace where they sent the money. They know our names. They know who has access to the account. They know who we are."

"And they still took the money?" Seth snorted. "They're not that smart if they know who we are and still took the money. Who all has access to the account?"

"Mom, Dad, Dezra, Me, Varg, and you."

"Me?"

Katrina shrugged as if it meant nothing that she'd given Seth access to the pride accounts. Her parents and his father all knew, and none of them had questioned it either.

"Well…yeah. You're the pride enforcer, right? You needed access to funds for hotel rooms, transportation, food…that kind of thing. Whatever you need on the hunt. How do you normally finance your rogue runs?"

"We never asked for money. We just used whatever we got from our percentage."

"Which is?"

"Forty-eight? I think? The house is free, and I'm not home enough to have many bills."

Katrina closed her eyes in frustration. "You hunt for smaller prides too, Seth—do you mean to say you put money into the accounts, but you never take anything out?" Katrina had set the account up to notify her when money was withdrawn but not when money was deposited. As far as she was concerned, it was only her business if her dad told her it was.

"The money in the account is for the pride. They need the funds. I have more than enough, and I don't need much. As far as I'm concerned, once I put it into the account, it doesn't exist anymore. Your dad makes sure the pride has what they need, and I do my part."

"You do your part by keeping them safe! You shouldn't be supporting your own hunts. Does my dad know?"

"He never told me how much to contribute. The guys and I just decided."

"And you don't even take a full half?"

Seth shrugged and immediately winced. "Like I said, we keep what we need and donate the rest for the pride."

"Seth... Darling...everyone contributes. It's not on you to make sure there is enough money. You're just supposed to be handling the rogue threats." She leaned in close to him and briefly dropped her forehead on his stomach, aggravated by his selfless acts. "There are four of you in your team, right? Are you splitting the forty-eight percent between the four of you?" Her voice was muffled against his bare skin.

"Twelve percent each," confirmed Seth, and his hand brushed her hair away from her face. "That's actually quite a bit sometimes."

"Sometimes..." Katrina groaned. "But even if—you shouldn't be having to dip into your personal pay for that. Give me your phone." She lifted her head and snatched his phone before he could respond, where she searched for the bank app she used and downloaded it to his phone. "Here. Sign in with your name and pick a password. When you need money for a room, or food, or whatever—that includes clothing replacements, paying vampires to erase human witnesses, and anything else you've had to shell out for, *use* the account! When you withdraw money, it'll show on the account that it was you. You can withdraw money from any ATM. Don't worry about explaining what it's for until you get back, and even then, I'm the one who keeps up with it, so I'll know what it was for."

Seth was quiet as he did what she instructed, his fingers tapping on the phone's screen as he came up with a password.

"And I'll know what you make your password—fair warning. I'm the primary account holder."

He grinned then. "Good. It's I Love You."

"If getting to an ATM becomes a problem when you're hunting, let me know, and I'll get you a card. Don't carry too much cash on you."

"It's really not that big of a deal—"

"It is to me. I put money into those accounts too. I do nothing else for the pride. You should at least be getting paid!"

"You being here is more than enough. I don't need money."

Katrina's heart constricted. "I almost got you killed."

"Since you came home, I haven't felt more alive in my entire life. Don't you understand, Kat? I just want you."

She groaned. Of course he'd say something that would set her entire body on fire when she couldn't even touch him without hurting him! Her gaze raked over his exposed chest and the ridge of his body beneath the blankets. He really was beautiful. Most of his flesh wounds were nearly gone now, thanks to his cat's superior healing skills, but the deeper ones remained. He wasn't bleeding anymore, thankfully, and she could tell he was still in quite a bit of pain, but he was a trooper and hadn't even complained once!

"That rib is going to take at least a couple days to heal," she muttered, distracted by the sight of so much of his flesh. She'd always been careful not to look at him too long, because she knew she'd give in if she had to deal with his heartbroken expression and his delicious body at the same time, both inviting her closer. Katrina knew he'd let her do anything she wanted to him, but what she wanted was for him to touch her. Too bad she'd led him up a mountain to be mauled by wild rogues. She frowned, considering what they could have been doing if she hadn't raced into the woods like a feral animal.

"I've been hurt worse, Kat. Calm down."

Katrina swallowed. She was feeling guilty, but not just because he was in pain. She'd been devouring him—in her mind anyway. She turned her gaze toward his, and she felt her cheeks burning with embarrassment.

He shifted, and his lips quirked into an uneven grin as he must've realized where her thoughts had been. "See something you're interested in, mate?"

Her throat burned as she struggled to respond. "You're healing nicely," she mumbled, unable to admit the truth.

"Mhm, the perks of being a shifter. Anything else you were thinking about?"

Katrina lifted her gaze to focus on the lamp that sat on the nightstand near the edge of the bed in an effort to avoid his stare. "I don't know what you're talking about."

"Sure you do. You know…it's only my ribs that are broken, not the rest of me."

"You have a punctured lung," gasped Katrina, and she leapt from the bed as if he'd just suggested she strip bare.

"Noooo, come back," teased Seth. He reached out with his uninjured arm, and he looked so pitiful that Katrina found herself easing back down onto the bed. She sat next to his hip, facing him, her face on fire as she forced herself to memorize every detail of his tufted headboard.

"Whatever you want, Kat, I'm game." His voice was low, filled with promise, and his intent had her stomach twisting into anxious knots.

"Your friends will be back any minute…"

"Mhm." He nodded.

"I need to call my dad and let him know we've been robbed. Again."

"Yep."

"I need to go get my laptop and see if my tracker worked."

"Yeah…"

Katrina moaned. "You know what you're doing to me. This isn't fair! I haven't the slightest clue what I'm doing! Emotionally broken, remember? I didn't exactly participate in the teenage rite of passage where we humped everything that moved, all right? You might have an idea of what you're doing, but I don't!" She slid off the bed once more and headed for the door.

"I'm sorry! I'll stop teasing. Please don't leave."

She paused halfway into the hall. That was the fourth time in the last thirty minutes that he'd begged her not to leave him, and she was starting to think he was serious. Did he think she wouldn't come back? Her cat screeched in protest and demanded she march right back into that bedroom and give as good as she got, but the human in her needed a second to breathe first.

Seth was far more alluring than she'd realized in her emotional stupor. If she'd had half a brain when he'd first approached her, she never would've been able to leave him for college, and she sure as hell wouldn't have stayed away so long. As a mature adult, she understood that if she'd stayed, they would've been happily mated by now, probably with half a dozen kids running around. The idea was not an unpleasant one—in fact, she could imagine it so perfectly that she knew if she stayed that was exactly what was going to happen anyway.

"Kat?" He couldn't see her standing outside his room debating her life choices, but he could likely still smell her and hear her racing heart.

"I'm getting my laptop," she mumbled. It wasn't a

lie. Her father had had someone deliver her bag as well as her suitcase earlier, and she was infinitely relieved that she wouldn't have to leave Seth alone to retrieve it—not to mention she knew her parents and Dezra would have questions, and she wasn't in the mood to answer them just yet.

****

Seth felt his pulse hammering in his ear as he waited, praying she'd come back. He knew he was taunting her, and she had no experience, but he couldn't help himself. He was letting his cat take the lead in hopes that he could convince her cat to give him the chance he'd always dreamt of. He knew deep in his heart that he could make her happy. He would make her a good mate. He just needed her to stick around long enough so he could show her.

Every time she moved away from him, tiny spurts of panic made him believe he'd scared her, and she would leave and never come back, just as he'd felt when she'd left for college all those years ago. He'd pacified himself then with the knowledge that she would eventually come back to visit her family, but he hadn't counted on her only coming around while he was gone. He didn't know he'd go so long without seeing her and inhaling her enticing scent. If he had, he would've followed her. He would have begged her for a chance. He sure as hell wouldn't have simply sat and waited! Seth understood her need for space, but he also understood that if he didn't act first, that she might never approach him, and his life had felt so meaningless without her.

Granted, it hadn't been a picnic while she had been around. It had been hell smelling her and knowing he couldn't do anything but watch her, because even if Kat hadn't been able to connect with her cat and feel the things he'd felt, her scent still called to him and demanded he make a move. She was still his mate. He still wanted her as desperately now as he had at sixteen.

Seth held his breath as he heard her steps on the carpet in the hallway, and he breathed a sigh of relief when she came back into the room carting her laptop bag. She tossed it on to the bed next to his knee and scowled at him. "You realize I'm not actually leaving, right? Like, I'm not going back to the city. I thought I made that clear?"

"You did." He struggled to contain the emotions his cat was spewing through his guts. His human heard her words, and they made sense in his head, but all the cat heard was leaving, and he wasn't in the right condition to calm the beast in that moment. He panicked, but he tried his best to hide it from her.

"I meant what I said. I agreed to move in with you, and I intend to…unless you changed your mind?"

One delicate eyebrow arched curiously as she stared down at him from the foot of the bed, and Seth nearly groaned. How was she so composed? He felt like his entire insides were being ripped out through his heart.

"I want you to stay." He said the words and forced himself to sound calm. "I need you to." He hoped his last words didn't sound as desperate as they felt, but he couldn't help it. If she left again, there would be no containing his cat a second time.

"Then stop looking at me like I'm breaking up with you. We're not even technically dating—are we?" Her eyes widened as if she only just realized her words.

Seth felt a moment of relief. "You belong with me in any capacity you're comfortable with." It took every ounce of his willpower to say those words, when all he really wanted was to claim her and make sure she never wanted to leave him ever again. His cat approved of this idea, and for an instant, Seth had complete control of himself.

"Then I could stay somewhere else...in town...as long as I'm close by?"

And just like that, he lost it again. How in the hell could she twist him into knots so easily? She kept complaining that things weren't fair, but she didn't even know the half of it. "Is it the house? You don't like it?" He wasn't even trying to hide his anxiety anymore. It was too much effort. "We can get a different house. Dezra can help you find something you like better. I'll live wherever you want."

She shook her head and crawled onto the bed, and if it had been possible for him to move without putting himself in intense pain, he would've been snatching her up in his arms and begging her to understand. Instead, he remained absolutely still and watched as she continued toward him, the picture of seduction. Her long blonde hair slid from her shoulders, and the front of her T-shirt hung low enough to give him a glimpse of her naked flesh inside. His gut clenched in anticipation, but she didn't stop. She crawled past her laptop and up toward him, her eyes flashing as she stared back at him.

Seth held his breath, and his lungs burned with the effort, but he didn't even care. If he passed out now, it would be with the image of his incredibly sexy mate crawling toward him on her hands and knees, the perfect arch of her back taunting him. She looked just like a damned cat right then, and if she hadn't known her effect on him before, then she couldn't miss it now. There was no way to hide the way her scent destroyed every bit of control he had, and if the heated scent of her desire wasn't enough, the picture of her crawling toward him had every bit of blood in his body rushing toward his groin. "Say something," he muttered, unable to keep the slight tremor from attacking both his hand and his voice.

Chapter Six

Katrina hadn't intended to tease her mate. Her original plan had been to reassure him of his place in her life, but the instant his human gaze had gone feline, it hadn't taken much for her to understand why. He was staring at her as if she were a fantasy come true, and despite her inexperience, his burning gaze made her feel like the world's most renowned seductress. Suddenly, every move she made felt like an invitation, and she wanted him to touch her.

He couldn't—she wouldn't let him. Not while he was still injured, but the instant he was better? Her blood sang through her veins, and her cat purred. Soon.

"Breathe, Seth." She slid onto the bed next to him and snuggled in close. She reached back and pulled her laptop bag into her lap and crossed her legs. "You can do whatever you want to me after you're better," she announced cheekily, not daring to look him in the eye. She withdrew her laptop from the bag and pushed it open. "What's the fun in losing my virginity to you now, when you can't even participate properly?"

She heard him exhale and felt her own cat-like grin in response. "I think I hear Luc and Lennix outside," she added, almost as an afterthought. "Is that going to be a problem?" She glanced pointedly at the ridge in the blanket between his thighs and forced her gaze to meet his. He was still staring at her through feline slits rather than human orbs, but he was at least breathing again.

"It isn't exactly something they haven't seen before…"

Katrina shrugged. "Well, if you don't mind—"

"I mind." He grabbed her laptop bag and placed it carefully over his hips, hiding his earlier reaction from prying eyes.

She smirked and twisted so that her back was against the pillows next to his head and began typing on the laptop keyboard as if it were the most normal thing in the world for her to be sitting next to him in bed, playing on her computer, while he lay completely naked, but for a blanket beside her. Maybe it was. It felt normal, anyway.

"So there are some things we should discuss," decided Katrina, uncaring if Luc and Lennix happened in on this particular conversation. She kept her gaze locked on the laptop screen in an effort to keep her courage from failing because she knew if she looked at him now it would be that much harder for her to discuss her concerns.

"The fact that you won't look at me makes me think I don't want to have this conversation," muttered Seth darkly.

"The fact that I won't look at you is because I'm a chicken, and I've never had a boyfriend, let alone a reason to discuss these particular topics, but they're important and need to be considered before I lose my nerve."

"Do I make you nervous, Kat?" He sounded surprised.

"Seth, you are absolutely terrifying—in the best way. If you could feel the way my heart bangs around inside my chest every time you smile at me, you'd understand why I have a hard time talking to you."

He lifted his hand and stroked his fingertips down her exposed forearm. "You don't need to be scared of me, mate. You own me—heart and soul. Nothing you say could make me love you any less. I have wanted you from the moment I met you."

"You were thirteen."

"And you were the prettiest girl in class. You stared at me with such big round green eyes, and I was lost from then on."

Katrina heard the front door open and knew Luc and Lennix would be interrupting any second, but it didn't matter. Their presence only reinforced her need to get all her thoughts and opinions out in the open, especially since they had a truce of sorts. Seth's friends needed to know she was as serious as he was, and the only way they'd believe that was if she were open and honest with Seth. She didn't want there to be any secrets.

"I've been thinking," began Katrina carefully as she brought the bank login screen up on her laptop. She needed the monotony of her work to keep her from losing her courage.

"Sounds dangerous," teased Lennix as he entered the room with a goofy grin and a bowl of whatever casserole Nia had concocted.

"Should we leave?" asked Luc as he followed suit, carrying two kitchen chairs with him into the room. He set them at the end of the bed as if he and his brother intended to be participants to whatever was about to occur between Katrina and Seth.

"Yes," hissed Seth.

"No." Katrina offered the brothers a friendly smile and invited them to sit. "He needs to eat."

"Kat," whined Seth.

"I wasn't going to say anything they can't hear too." Katrina shrugged and studied the laptop in front of her. She could nearly do this in her sleep, which was fortunate because she wasn't a bit focused.

"You heard the lady—eat." Lennix shoved a bowl of food in Seth's direction, and Katrina was relieved when he took it, albeit a bit grudgingly.

Luc left and returned with two more bowls, one of which he set on the table at Katrina's elbow. The other he took to one of the chairs at the end of the bed and made himself comfortable.

Lennix darted out of the room and returned carting his own bowl as well as several bottles of water, which he tossed on the bed, then plopped down onto the second chair next to his brother. "What life altering discussion are we having now?"

Katrina rolled her eyes. "Not life altering exactly, just questions." The smell of hot tuna and melted cheese invaded her senses, but she didn't so much as pause over the keyboard. She needed to track a thief and discuss the rest of her life with her mate. No big deal.

"Mhm, and the laptop?" asked Luc, less concerned with Seth's love life.

"Someone has sticky fingers. We have a thief hacking into the pride's secondary account and skimming off the top," explained Seth with a growl. "Ward gave us permission to handle it, but Katrina's the computer whiz, and we need to know where we're going. She's trying to track the thief."

Lennix whistled. "First a rogue, now a thief. You're moving up in the world, princess."

Katrina smirked. "Your team—excluding Seth, will be doing the dirty work. I'm only pointing you in the right direction."

"If this takes longer than a couple days, Seth will be good enough to go too," argued Luc.

"Oh, boy, please! This won't even take an hour!"

"Did I miss something?" huffed Seth. "Are you three friends now?"

"We bonded over your half-dead body," chirped Lennix. He grinned as he shoved a bit of cooked pasta into his mouth. "We decided we like her."

"We did?" Luc raised one eyebrow.

"Well I like her." Lennix smirked.

Seth growled low, the sound more animal than man. "Bonded how?"

Katrina paused long enough to pat Seth's shoulder reassuringly. "So, I can't track the account to get the money back, but I was able to install a virus so that anyone who accesses it will be going home with a bug in their system."

Luc sighed in defeat. "Ok, I'm impressed. I like you too. What else?"

She smirked but didn't look away from the laptop screen. It was a nice feeling having someone other than Seth interested in her wellbeing—her family excluded of course.

"Hold on. I need to know what happened while I was unconscious," huffed Seth.

"You mostly just bled a lot," admitted Lennix. "Your dad and the alpha came. Katrina lost her shit…"

"Lennix made her cry," supplied Luc.

89

"You what?!" Seth attempted to sit up and snarled in frustration when his pain forced him to lie back again.

"Betrayal," gasped Lennix.

"I said she was at least a top five, YOU said she was hot," argued Luc.

"Hold the hell on, WHAT?" Seth shifted once more.

"You're making it sound worse than it was," muttered Katrina absently. "And I did not lose my shit. I was reasonably overwhelmed. After all, I fought a rogue and lived to tell about it, and I'm not even trained! I only learned to defend myself from spying on—" She paused, and her face began to burn as the brothers focused on her once more.

Seth grinned.

"Wait, is there a rated R version?" gasped Lennix with a teasing grin.

Kat rolled her eyes once more. She couldn't help it. "If there was, I wouldn't tell you." She shrugged, brushing off her embarrassment the best she could.

"That means yes," snickered Lennix.

"Her dad had her suitcases delivered to your living room," announced Luc.

"Really?" Seth grinned.

"We have a thief to discuss," interrupted Katrina, determined to direct the conversation away from her awkward childhood. "And your friends and I have an understanding."

"She has custody during the week, and we get to see you on the weekends. We share Sunday every other week," announced Lennix.

"Don't forget the holidays," agreed Luc with a

chuckle.

Katrina giggled but kept her gaze on the laptop.

"Told you she'd like my jokes," hissed Lennix. "You owe me twenty dollars."

"Considering that's the first time I've ever heard her laugh, she probably doesn't even know what a good joke actually sounds like," muttered Luc, but he tucked his hand into his back pocket and came away with a twenty-dollar bill, which he shoved at his brother.

As much as she was enjoying their banter, Katrina couldn't help but regret all the time she'd wasted becoming an emotionless robot. If she'd only understood how to get along with her cat, she could've made friends long before now, and she wouldn't have had to rely on Seth to make her different. She doubted he minded, he was grinning after all, but it still hurt to imagine what her life could've been like—if only.

"The thief lives in the city," proclaimed Katrina. Her fingers flew across the keyboard, retracing the hacker's steps through her own firewall until she could identify the first couple numbers of the IP address on the computer that was used to steal their money. With or without the IP, the bug would be able to identify the thief's address in a matter of hours. It was just a matter of narrowing it down to a street and house number. Already, Katrina knew the state and district, which is how she knew the hacker lived in the city close to where Katrina herself had resided.

"Great—you said you had questions for Seth, and I *have* to hear them," decided Lennix as he finished his dinner. He leaned forward and snatched one of the bottled waters from the end of the bed.

Katrina nodded. "How many kids do you want,

Seth?"

Seth choked on a bite of his casserole.

"I've given it a bit of thought, and if I hadn't been so messed up, we would've gotten together, and I wouldn't have gone off to college and hid in the city. You and I would've had kids by now, so how many do you think we would have?" Katrina tried to make her question sound as clinical as possible, but her heart was threatening to beat out of her chest.

"At least ten," proclaimed Lennix. "As much as he obsessed over you, I'm going to assume he would've kept you pregnant."

"You're not accounting for twins, which runs in his family," said Luc with a shrug.

"You're really staying, then?" asked Seth softly.

"I did say that," huffed Katrina. "More than once."

"And you did run off to the city and refuse to see me for an entire decade," argued Seth.

"I did say I love you, as well."

Seth grinned. "You did say that too…"

"Right, so the thief lives somewhere close to where I did, and I know you all knew where I was, because there's no way my father would've let me leave without having at least a couple of you stalking me, even if he does trust the locals to keep an eye on me."

"Not us. Team two was on Princess detail. We strictly hunt rogues," explained Luc.

"Technically…that's not true. They take volunteers occasionally. I went once. I knew where she was," admitted Lennix. He sent Seth a meaningful look. "She rejected you! I had to make sure she wasn't screwing around."

Seth opened his mouth to respond, but Katrina beat

him to it. "You're right. But I wouldn't have cheated. I rejected him, not the other way around. It wasn't his fault, and it wouldn't have been right." She shrugged and continued tapping on the keyboard as if one of the most important conversations of her life wasn't happening. "Aside from that, the reason I rejected him was still relevant until a few hours ago, so I wasn't interested in that sort of thing anyway."

"Right, that's what the guys said. You never went out with friends, never even made friends, didn't do anything but go to class and go home. The only time you left was to drop paintings off at a local gallery. And the guy who dealt with them was gay—I checked." Lennix seemed unapologetic as he described the last few years of her life down to a T.

"There was no point in making friends when I could not allow myself to care about them." Finally, as Katrina admitted the truth, the screen flashed with the exact address of the thief. The building directly across from the one Katrina had lived in. She didn't know which apartment number, but the IP address was still loading, and until they had proof, they couldn't very well confront a random stranger. "As soon as I get this number, you'll be good to go." She watched the numbers changing on the screen as the program cycled through the possible options. "There!" The IP address of the computer used to steal their funds flashed on the screen, and Katrina quickly whipped her phone out to text them to Seth. "You can forward that to your teammates. It has the address and the IP address."

"We don't know anything about computers. How are we going to know if we have the right one?" asked Lennix.

"Call Seth. I'll walk you through it," said Katrina confidently. "All you have to do is bring up the search engine and type IP address, and the results will tell you. You just have to make certain the computer is logged onto the internet. If the number matches the one Seth sends you, then that's our guy."

"What if there's more than one person in the house? How do we know which one it was?" asked Luc.

"You hunt rogues. Nothing is scarier than that. I'm sure you can figure something out." Katrina closed the laptop and slid it onto the bed.

"Are you giving us permission to torture them?" Lennix's gaze grew wide. "As the alpha's daughter, you could."

"I'm giving you permission to do whatever Seth decides is necessary. He's your leader, not me."

"Seth won't be there," said Luc quietly.

"And neither will I," responded Katrina.

Chapter Seven

Lyndra couldn't take it anymore. She'd been pretending to hack into the cat's bank account for hours to avoid admitting to the assholes in her living room that she'd already gotten the job done. She knew what would happen the instant she did what they wanted.

Frustrated, she stood and shoved her chair away from the computer desk. She was still wearing her pajamas as she had been the day her sister stumbled into the apartment bloody and bruised after having told the males accompanying her sister about Lyndra's talents.

Celina was only sixteen and had been flirting with a pack of wolves across town for weeks. Lyndra had warned her that they were no good and advised her sister to stay away from them, but Celina hadn't listened. She'd bragged about Lyndra's computer skills in an effort to impress them, and the wolves had predictably reacted the way Lyndra had known they would. They'd shown up with a half-dead Celina in their grasp, and Lyndra had been forced to do whatever they said in order to keep her sister alive.

"Feed the damned baby," screeched Lyndra as she whirled into the living room angrily. Sixteen-year-old Celina was hardly conscious in a dog kennel near the door where they'd locked her in to keep her from escaping, and Lyndra's six-month-old sister lay crying in her crib near Lyndra's bedroom door. It had been just the three of them for over a week now, since the wolves had killed Lyndra's parents. Not that her parents had been the best to begin with. They often left Lyndra and her sisters alone for weeks on end, showing up to eat whatever food Lyndra had managed to collect before leaving again. It had been months since Lyndra had talked to an actual adult, and she'd been taking care of her baby sister for nearly as long.

"Get my money and I will," snarled the male wolf. He wasn't a rogue, which was both fortunate and unfortunate as well. If he'd been rogue, Lyndra could've killed him, she had the right, but if he'd been rogue, he'd likely have killed them first. He didn't belong to any pack, but there were four others in his group who hung out beneath the bridge where Celina had found her boyfriend—the man who'd beat the shit out of her and now threatened Lyndra and their baby sister as well. He'd played Celina right into the palm of his hand, gotten what he wanted from her, and was currently holding the three of them hostage demanding the money Celina had assured him Lyndra could collect.

Lyndra scowled at the man. He wasn't much older than Celina was, which was a shame, because he might've made a good mate if he wasn't so damned evil! He was definitely strong enough to defend his family and was honestly good looking in a broody, rugged sort of way. He was only eighteen, however, and he'd been kicked out of his pack for reasons Lyndra didn't have to wonder about. His comrades weren't much older. The eldest was maybe in his early twenties, and they had all belonged to the same pack, but as far as she could tell, they weren't related.

"Feed my sister or there will be no money!"

"Get my money or your sister isn't going to need to eat!"

Lyndra flinched. She recognized the threat for what it was. He would kill them all, and she doubted the city runners would even care. They'd never shown any interest in the girls before. They weren't human, and as far as she could tell, the hunters only cared about protecting humans, not three lowly foxes.

"Feed her!"

"Money!"

"If you want me to get your money, then the baby has to be fed! I can't concentrate with all her screaming!"

"I could get rid of her now. Then you wouldn't have to worry about her crying!"

Lyndra shuddered. She'd never in her life been so angry. "I will feed her, and if you so much as lay a single hand on either of my sisters, I will report you to the hunters."

"We're not rogue, sweetie. They won't give a shit," taunted Celia's ex-boyfriend.

"Then I'll make sure the cats you're robbing know exactly where their money went."

The wolf's gaze grew dark as he glowered at her. "You tell those feline bastards who I am, and I'll slit your throat, little girl." He took a threatening step toward her. "Get my damned money—NOW!"

Without a word, Lyndra stomped past the wolf and into the kitchen where she snatched a bottle and filled it with warm water, then measured in a serving of formula. She was shaking it quietly when she marched past him a second time, snatching the diaper bag on her way to the crib, where she gently collected her crying sister and carted her into their shared bedroom, where Lyndra made herself comfortable in her computer chair once more and began typing on the keyboard with her free hand while she fed the baby with the other, her arm wrapped awkwardly around the hungry infant, so that the wolves would think she was still trying to hack into the cat's bank account. They wanted far more money than Lyndra was prepared to steal. She knew they wouldn't stop with the cats, however. It was more likely they'd keep her around, hacking into whoever's account she could get into. Her heart hurt at the thought, but at least for now her sister wasn't crying anymore.

Celia still moaned in pain, but there wasn't much Lyndra could do for her. She would be fine, their shifter DNA would see to it, but their little sister wouldn't be if she didn't eat.

****

"I should be with them." Seth scowled at his phone and listened as his team surrounded the apartment building where the hacker who'd taken their money was still presumably inside.

Meanwhile, Katrina continued to hammer away on her keyboard, and she'd managed to hack into the apartment building's security cameras. He could see his team moving quietly through the halls, but he wouldn't be able to see inside the thief's room.

"And you would've been if I hadn't nearly gotten you killed." Katrina's quiet voice rang with guilt, and he reached out toward her.

"Stop blaming yourself. You did nothing wrong.

We were just at the wrong place at the wrong time. It could've easily been one of our pride mates who'd wondered too far into the mountain—a child even. We saved someone else's life by being there. If I'd sensed the second one before I hit the first, I would've been better prepared, and I would've been able to handle the situation. I screwed up—not you."

He felt her relax under his touch and sighed in relief. "Focus on the guys, they need direction. They've never been on a hunt without me before."

Katrina nodded, and he watched her square her shoulders. His brave beautiful mate—he adored her. She didn't understand how much she meant to him, but he was committed to spending the rest of his life showing her, especially now that he knew she was in fact staying with him. Permanently. Suddenly all those lonely nights were worthwhile, just for these moments he'd been able to talk with her.

"I've been monitoring the accounts since the guys left," began Katrina as she shifted through the various windows on her laptop. Her gaze flew across the screen as fast as her fingers on the keyboard, and Seth was struck with awe. She was amazing, and she didn't even seem to know it. It boggled his mind that she was so clueless about her own worth and made him wish he'd tried harder to get through to her when he'd had the chance. He'd doubted himself and thought she simply thought less of him too, but he'd been wrong. There wasn't a prejudiced bone in Katrina's whole body.

"And? Your tone implies something's wrong…"

"Not wrong…different. The hacker made themselves a profile on our account and gave themselves access."

"What?! How is that even possible without your permission?"

"She knows my password, and I can't change it while she's in the system."

"She?"

Katrina nodded. "Her profile says Lyndra Osyn."

"But you can see her password, right? You're still administrator?"

His mate nodded once more. "It's HELP, in all capital letters. She knows I'm watching her. She knows we're coming."

The second screen flashed, and Katrina moved her mouse toward the video of the apartment security feed, where Seth's guys had finally located the apartment and busted in. Seth could hear the shouts of alarm and snarling and knew their opponents were not mere humans.

"What's happening?" gasped Katrina. "There are no cameras in the apartment for me to access. I can't get past the doorway."

Seth brought his phone up so they could hear whatever was coming through on Luc's phone but it did nothing to provide them video. "We should've fitted them with cameras," muttered Seth.

The sound of a baby crying interrupted his thoughts, and his wide-eyed gaze swung to Katrina's, who looked just as stunned.

"Is that…a baby?" She stared at her laptop hard as if she could make it show her what was happening inside the thief's room.

"The girl," shouted Luc, and the phone went silent.

"He shifted," sighed Seth in frustration. "His phone is in the nether with his clothes."

"There was a baby. I know what a baby sounds like. And why would he shift unless they weren't human? Who the hell is Lyndra Osyn?" Katrina's fingers flew over the keyboard, searching, and her skin paled as the image of a thirteen-year-old child showed on the screen. "She's a damn kid? Our thief is a child!" She began typing once more, and Seth was flabbergasted by how fast she was able to find the information she needed. "Why would a kid need twenty thousand dollars? Why wouldn't she just take it all? This doesn't make sense…"

Seth was quiet as he watched her answer her own questions. "I'm in touch with the city patrol. They say she's a shifter—a fox…they're on their way to help the guys now…they have no idea what's going on either." Katrina groaned. "If I'd known…"

"You couldn't have."

"Three pissed off feline shifters just broke into her family's house—they must be so scared!"

"Relax, Katrina. They wouldn't hurt a kid. She sent you a message, right? Help? You said she knew we were coming. Maybe she was just trying to get our attention."

"I should've gone with them…"

"You're not trained."

Seth watched his mate grow even more frustrated as Luc's phone remained silent.

"I've lost contact with the city patrol too."

Seth's own heart sank. "Everything's going to be fine, Katrina. Just give them some time. Can you hack her computer webcam from here?"

Katrina's gaze focused on his. "Yes!" She immediately began typing once more, and Seth watched as boxes of information appeared and she put in a series of numbers and commands that went far beyond what he could comprehend, but after a few moments, a picture appeared of a young girl's bedroom. It was trashed and a thirteen-year-old girl clutched a screaming baby to her chest. Tears streamed down her face, and she looked absolutely terrified. Her door was closed, but she flinched as something hit it hard and smashed it open.

For an instant, Luc, in his cat form was visible as he clashed with a young wolf, but then they were gone again, and the girl was squatting down beside her bed, still trying to protect the infant.

"Can we talk to her?"

"I can't find a mic on her computer. It's an older model and frankly a piece of shit. I don't even know how she managed to get into our account with those outdated programs. She's even stealing WiFi from her neighbors." Katrina scowled at the monitor. "This kid took twenty thousand dollars from us, but I highly doubt she had a choice."

"You said she was a fox, right? Luc was fighting a wolf—"

"None of this makes sense! Why is there a baby? Where are her parents?"

Katrina gasped as a male human body came flying at the computer knocking it to the ground. The screen shuddered and darkened, but despite being knocked to the floor, the webcam was still broadcasting, and rather than the kid hiding behind the bed, they could see out through the doorway and into the living room where all hell had broken loose.

Mountain lions and wolves fought viciously,

destroying what bit of furniture there was, while another young girl crouched inside a large dog kennel. She was covered in bruises and dried blood and looked just as terrified as the one holding the baby.

Seth's heart practically exploded in his chest at the sight. "Holy hell!"

Katrina gasped tearfully. "They're all just kids…"

They watched as Luc was knocked to the ground, and the wolf he'd been fighting shot across the room and changed back into his human self. He unlatched the kennel and jerked the girl out of the opening. He held her shaking body against his and said something, but Seth couldn't read lips. He could only assume that it was something to the nature of killing the girl if Luc followed them.

Seth knew Luc wouldn't risk the girl's life, and he grudgingly let the wolf leave through the front door with the girl still held in the rogue's grip. Feet appeared at the bottom of the screen, blocking their view, but within minutes new shifters had arrived to help contain the two remaining wolves, and there wasn't a rogue among them. Suddenly, the monitor went dark.

"He took her," whispered Katrina in shock. "That asshole wolf took that girl!"

"We'll get her back," promised Seth.

****

Katrina paced the bedroom floor at the foot of Seth's bed and knew if there'd been carpet it would be threadbare by now. "We should put pants on you," she blurted suddenly. No doubt when the guys arrived back her father would bring the girls to Katrina to talk one on one. One computer genius to another.

"In the closet." Seth's response was brisk and not

at all the smooth cozy cat he'd been up until that point. He was worried. She could see it in his eyes.

Katrina hadn't realized when she fished a pair of loose jogging pants from his dresser that she would be the one putting them on him, but as she stood at the end of his bed, with his pants in her hand, she stared at him cautiously as if he might suddenly come up off the bed and bite her.

He stared back at her, but his human stare had gone feline once more, and he was watching her with a half-lidded gaze and a knowing grin that was comparable to a cat who'd caught the canary. He knew she was struggling, and he didn't offer to help her. Nearly all of his flesh wounds had healed in the hours since the attack, but broken bones would take days, and they couldn't risk him puncturing his lung again. They needed him in the field.

Katrina brought her hands toward her face nervously and immediately realized her mistake when she inhaled a deep breath of his scent on the pants she was still clutching. She felt her own pupils narrow to sharp vertical slits and swallowed. He was injured. That was the only reason she wasn't naked under him. The fact was both exciting and terrifying.

Seth Mourgent was a woman's wet dream, and he was hers for the taking. He was staring at her as if she already was naked, while she was standing at the foot of the bed like a teenage virgin who'd never seen a boy without his clothes before. Technically, other than being nearly thirty, the rest was true enough, she decided. As a shifter, she'd seen men naked before on plenty of occasions. Nudity wasn't a big deal with their animal natures, but she'd never seen Seth naked before, and somehow it was a big deal to her.

"I…um…" She struggled to form words as her gaze raked over his partially covered body, and she watched incredulously as his body reacted in kind. "I tried not to look earlier when I cleaned all the blood off," she admitted. It was mostly true. He also hadn't been awake watching her. It made a difference.

"Why? You're allowed to look as much as you want, Kat. I'm yours." His cat-like gaze never left her face, even as she took a few cautious steps toward him.

"I feel like I have ten years of emotions raging through me, and I can't process them all at once," she admitted breathlessly. "I feel sixteen again, and you're the cutest guy I've ever seen—you keep smiling at me, and my heart just does this little flippy thing that I can't understand."

"My heart has been doing that little flippy thing since the day I met you." Seth's grin was infectious, and Katrina couldn't help but smile back at him.

"Then you say things like that, and all I can think about is sinking my fangs into your skin and making you mine for the rest of my life."

His heated gaze slid down her body and back up again. "Do it. I've been waiting for so long."

"I don't know what I'm doing," she whispered as she took another step toward him, where he still lay unmoving on the bed.

"No one does. Just keep doing whatever it is with me. That's the key." She could see his stomach muscles clenching as he struggled to keep his breathing under control, and she knew she was teasing him, but it was completely unintentional, and she didn't know how not to. The cat in her was ecstatic. She was finally getting what she'd wanted for so long, and Katrina wasn't trying to stop her anymore.

"Once you're healed…"

His lazy gaze turned hot. "There are things I can do that don't involve me moving, Kat."

"For now, pants. In a couple days…" She left her intentions unsaid.

He had to know very well what she was implying, and his teasing gaze left no room for misunderstandings in her mind.

"Pants, then."

Katrina held her breath as she reached for the blanket covering him and tugged it slowly down his body, revealing more and more of his agonizingly gorgeous skin. She tried not to look him in the eye as she bent to help him slide his naked legs into the pants, but she could feel his gaze on her, unwavering as she moved over him, sliding the jogging pants up over his thighs and finally his hips. Every part of her was on fire, from her cheeks to her thighs, but the cat was purring so loudly Katrina forgot to be embarrassed.

"Does it still hurt when you breathe?" she asked softly as she crawled over him to settle on the bed next to him.

"I think the puncture is mostly healed. It's tender, but the ribs are the most painful."

Katrina nodded, her mind already forming a plan of attack. "Now that we know the guys are safe and they won't be back for a bit, I feel much better."

"You're trying to distract me."

"I'm deciding."

"On?"

She sat back on her heels and lifted her T-shirt up

over her head and tossed it onto the floor next to the bed.

He hissed in response, and she grinned. "What about now? Does it hurt to breathe?"

"No more than it did before."

Katrina sucked her bottom lip between her teeth nervously and let her gaze travel over his body. From the outside he looked fine. A few puckered pink scars littered his body, reminders from this morning's attack, but she could see the slight misshapen curve beneath his chest and still hear the slight wheeze when he took a deep breath. "I think there are some things we can do that shouldn't hurt…if you're willing."

"So willing," he gasped.

She lifted her hand toward his stomach with an amused grin and watched the muscles tighten beneath her fingertips. He was quiet as she traced the curve of his body up over his shoulder. The skin was still bruised, but she leaned over him and massaged gently. "Tell me if I hurt you," whispered Katrina.

"Kat…" Seth's response was something between a gasp and a purr. "I've dreamt about this so many times."

"I haven't done anything yet," chuckled Katrina.

"You're here, in my bed, half naked. That's farther than I ever thought I'd get. Anything else is just…magic."

She rolled her eyes with a grin. "Before you released my cat, I would've argued that this has nothing to do with magic. Biology, nature, chemical reaction…" She smirked. "But the cat knows there's more to this than that. There is a bond that cannot be broken. I don't have years of pent-up frustrations to release on you, but

I do have new, undiscovered feelings and emotions that I've never felt before that I know I'll never feel with anyone else. You're going to have to be content with that, because until you're better, that's all you get."

"That is more than enough, Kat. I'll take everything I can get with you." His voice was rough as he reached out for her. "I need you closer."

Katrina slid farther up on the bed and ran her fingers across his collar bone. "I painted you once, but it didn't do you justice. The real you is so much better than the one I kept in my mind."

He lifted his hand to her hip and caressed her skin. "I'm sure you did amazing."

"It wasn't you."

"Nothing is as good as the real thing; my dreams did not compare to the way you feel in my arms." His hand slipped down and around toward her upper thigh. "I want to touch you so badly."

Katrina sat back, giving him access to whatever part of her he wanted to touch. "You have until the guys get back."

"Then keep the rest of your clothes on, because you're not going to have time to get dressed again before they're outside our door."

His promises were enough to have every nerve in her body humming with anticipation. "As long as you don't hurt yourself," she gasped as his fingers traveled even farther up her thigh. His exploring touch didn't stop between her thighs where she'd expected him to, but slid higher, up her bare stomach, to cup first one bra-clad breast, and then the other, before he was caressing the curve of her belly once more. "You mentioned kids, and now I can't stop imagining your belly round and full with our child."

Katrina closed her eyes, unable to respond as the mental image he created filled her mind.

"I imagine busting my ass all day to make sure you're safe, then coming home to you every night and burying myself inside you until I can't think straight. I've thought of almost nothing else since you left for college, and no amount of missing you has changed my mind."

Katrina inhaled a sharp breath of relief as his hand finally made it back down between her thighs, and he ran his fingers along her panty line. She'd changed into comfortable pajama shorts earlier after her shower, knowing that she'd be lounging around until he was back on his feet, but now she wished she hadn't even put those on. They were most definitely in her way. She wiggled to give him better access, and he chuckled.

"I love you, Kat, so damned much." His voice was low and filled with promise. "I can't wait to spend the rest of my life with you." He purred, and Katrina felt a shiver slice through her at the seductive sound. She shifted carefully to avoid nudging his broken ribs, and he tugged her panties to the side. "Tell me you love me too, Kat. I keep thinking this is just another dream, and I'll wake up and you'll be gone."

Katrina gasped as his fingers made contact with her burning flesh. "I do, more than you can ever understand." Her response was a breathy rasp, and she arched into his touch as he began to play her like a well-tuned instrument. As many times as she'd done this on her own, it had never felt like this. She'd always treated herself like a machine that occasionally needed to be oiled, but with her cat in the game, things were so much more. Katrina had no idea the proper way to explain the way he made her feel, but she wanted to keep feeling it for the rest of her life and beyond if possible.

Chapter Eight

Luc Darther knew the instant that son-of-a-bitch wolf ran out the door with the teenage girl his brother would lose his shit. Lennix could not handle seeing kids hurt, and this mission was bad from the start, but the instant they'd walked into the apartment where the supposed thief was, it had only gotten worse. Not only was their thief a thirteen-year-old child, but she was also a shifter and worse, she and her sisters were alone.

Luc had smelled the sick scent of death the instant he'd walked in, and he knew without looking what he'd find in the bathroom. Even Lennix, whose nose wasn't nearly as good as some shifters, knew, and it had only made everything worse. They'd planned for a quick, easy, quiet in and out, but they hadn't been prepared for the shit storm inside the apartment.

Four nasty wolves had destroyed the tiny apartment. They'd eaten every bit of food the three girls had left, and they'd clearly hurt the girl locked in a cage. Luc's own temper had gone from zero to sixty real damn quick, but it was nothing compared to Lennix, who'd shifted the instant he saw those kids and lunged straight for the first wolf's throat. It was all Luc could do to keep his brother from going full cat, even though he was having a hard-enough time controlling his own beast.

Within minutes of entering the apartment, it

became crystal clear what was going on, and Luc had had no choice but to shift and take on the wolves. As a result, he'd lost contact with his leader. He let his instincts lead him, and he killed one of the bastard wolves, but at least two others had escaped, including the one who took the girl.

Lennix was still in his cat form when the city patrol arrived to help, but Luc knew they wouldn't be able to help much other than with clean up and to bribe any humans who'd heard the fight. Ironically, no one had come to investigate, but then it seemed like the entire apartment building was screaming at one another, so they probably just hadn't heard the four wolves and three mountain lions snarling at each other. It was a miracle, and one Luc didn't question. With Katrina on their side, there would be no video footage either, which made everything slightly easier, but it didn't help him find the young girl who'd been taken.

After nearly thirty minutes, Lennix finally shifted back, but it was clear to Luc that he wasn't himself yet. He bounced on the balls of his feet, his hands clenched in fists as he stared at the bathroom door, almost as if in a trance.

Luc walked past him and patted his back. "We'll take care of them. They're safe now," he vowed to his brother, but he didn't know exactly what he'd promised. All that mattered was making sure Lennix didn't go after the last two wolves. They had to be smart or they'd get that poor girl killed.

Instead, Luc walked quietly past the chaos left in the living room and headed for the bedroom where he found two fox kits—the thirteen-year-old who'd robbed them, and a screaming baby in her arms. They stared at him with wide almond-shaped eyes and jet-black hair, and they were nearly identical. "We need to know everything," he said gently, not wanting to startle the girl. There was an open window next to her, and he was half afraid she'd try to jump if he approached her.

The girl sobbed and clutched the baby tighter in her arms, which made the little one scream louder. "I'm so sorry," cried the girl. "Please don't hurt us. I didn't have a choice!"

Luc nodded. "I know. We're not here to hurt you...we came to help." He took a cautious step toward the two children. "Are your parents—" He couldn't say the words.

She nodded solemnly.

"Okay...okay." Luc felt his own heart clench. "All right. We can handle this, right? You know who I am, don't you?"

"One of the cats. I stole your money. I'm so sorry!"

"I don't care about that. You sent our friend a message. You asked for help?"

The girl nodded. "They were going to make me keep taking more. Please, don't hurt my sister. She was stupid, but she didn't mean to hurt anyone."

"The other girl?"

The thirteen-year-old nodded tearfully.

"What's your name, kid?"

"Lyndra Osyn. This is my sister Ema. I named her." Lynda continued to clutch the crying baby. "She's hungry."

Luc nearly cried. "Let's get her fed, then. Grab her things. We'll take you somewhere safe."

Lyndra hesitated. "Are you going to kill us? I'm sorry I took your money— it wasn't for us. They made me do it. Please, you have to believe me!"

"I do." Luc swallowed past the knot in his throat. He knew if it was this hard for him to hear what happened, then Lennix would be losing his shit soon. "Look, why don't we get you and the baby taken care of, and then we'll find your sister."

"Find her?" Lyndra's eyes widened even more. "Where did she go?"

"The wolf took her, but don't worry! We're gonna get her back. We just have to be careful about it."

Lyndra shifted the crying baby. "Swear you won't hurt us, and I'll know if you're lying!"

Luc's gaze softened. "Of course you will know. You're a shifter too, aren't you, little fox?" He grinned encouragingly and watched as her terrified expression faded to relief. "My pride will take care of you."

"Even though I took your money?"

"Even though." Luc was confident in his vow. He knew his alpha would never hold such a thing against the child. Even if Lyndra hadn't been thirteen, their alpha was a kind man who would see that she wasn't to blame. The wolves, however. Luc expected that his team would be going on a rogue hunt soon, even if the rogues they hunted weren't exactly rogues at all. There was no excuse for what they'd done, and Luc would see that they paid for what they'd done to these children. "Come with me?"

Lyndra nodded and grabbed a diaper bag from the edge of her bed. She shouldered the bag and shifted the baby in her arms. "There's formula in the kitchen. We can feed her in the car."

Luc snapped his fingers, knowing his team could hear every word. Without hesitation, Gossom, typically the fourth member of their team, jumped to attention and went to the kitchen to retrieve the baby's bottle and formula.

"Fill it with warm water, not hot," instructed Lyndra. "Measure in two scoops of that formula and give it a good shake."

Luc's heart ached to hear the girl speak as if she were the child's mother. It was clear that she had been taking care of this baby for a long while, and it made him wonder about their parents. He knew they were dead, but what about before the wolves had arrived? He couldn't stomach the thought of what the fox kits had gone through, and he didn't dare ask. They'd likely need therapy. Thankfully, their pride had one such female that was amazing with children, and once Katrina talked to them, Luc would personally make sure the girls made it to Lacy Baraek's house. He owed her a visit anyway after what she'd done to help Lennix the last time kids had been involved in their mission.

As Luc led the skittish foxes past his brother, he latched onto Lennix 's arm and pulled him out the door too. Gossom was close behind, and as a group they left the city patrol to deal with the mess they'd made. It didn't occur to Luc that Seth and Katrina were still waiting on him to call until they were miles away in the team SUV heading back toward his pride's territory.

Nearly three hours later Luc parked the SUV outside Seth's house and waited for his brother to step out too, leaving Gossom in the car with the two children.

"Are you okay, Lennix? Do you need to see Lacy again?"

His brother scowled at the ground. "I'm fine. I'll be

115

at Nia's."

Luc sighed. "You can't get drunk every time something bad happens."

"Like hell I can't." Lennix stalked away from the car and headed back down the street where he'd eventually find his way to Nia's bar.

"Lennix, we'll find the other girl! You have to trust me!"

His twin didn't respond but kept walking. Luc sighed. He couldn't control his brother, and he sure as hell couldn't promise they'd find the other girl alive. But he would find her. For the moment, Luc had to consider their mission a success or it would eat at him the way it did Lennix, and that was the last thing these kids needed. With Seth out of commission for a couple more days and Lennix losing his shit, it was just him and Gossom, and that was not a mission he was looking forward to heading. Two feral wolves against two cats with a young female fox involved? It sounded like hell. With any luck the alpha would assign a second team to help him because Luc seriously doubted he could handle it all on his own without at least Seth, even if Lennix didn't come back any time soon.

They were used to Lennix skipping out for a few days any time kids were involved. They expected it. It was something he couldn't help. Luc knew it had to do with their own abusive childhood, and he didn't blame his brother one bit, but Luc also knew of all times, this was one when he needed Lennix to keep it together, at least long enough to rescue the third sister.

****

Seth was a content house cat. He felt like one anyway. Katrina was sporting his mating mark, and though he hadn't gotten hers yet, he knew she was only waiting for him to heal. They were as good as mated, and his cat was in feline heaven. After so many years of waiting, she was finally his in every way, and he was nearly purring when he heard the SUV pull up his driveway.

"They're back," gasped Katrina, and she rushed out of his room to let them in.

Seth would've liked to have met them at the door as well, but as it was shifter DNA was fast, but it wasn't that fast. Instead, he'd managed to sit up in bed, and he at least had pants on now, but he was no closer to getting out of bed on his own than he had been that morning.

He heard footsteps on the stairs, and Kat appeared with Luc and a young girl in tow. "This is our hacker," said Kat, her tone filled with pride. "Isn't she amazing?" Kat's eyes lit up, and Seth could only grin at the sight of her. She was practically glowing, and despite the circumstances, she was in awe of the girl who'd stolen twenty thousand dollars from them. It was the strangest thing, but he was oddly proud of the girl's skills too, even if she had used them to steal.

"He promised you wouldn't be mad at me," whispered the girl cautiously, her dark almond-shaped eyes full of fear. "I told the truth—I swear I wouldn't have done it if I had a choice."

Seth nodded understandingly. Luc had filled them in on most of the situation, but he knew his teammate had left a few things out that they'd discuss once the girls were safe. "I heard you had a little sister?"

The girl nodded. "We left Ema with your alpha. His mate promised to take good care of her while we talked."

"Ema? That's a nice name. How old is she?"

"Six months I think." She shrugged. "My mother dropped her off a few days after she was born. I don't actually know when her birthday is. We—Celina and I just started calling her Ema. We don't even know what mom named her."

Seth opened his mouth to ask the obvious question, but Luc gave a quick shake of his head, and he took the hint for what it was. "And the wolves?"

"Celina was dating one of them. He was an asshole. I tried to tell her to stay away from him, but she thinks she's the boss and I don't know what I'm talking about." The girl rolled her eyes in much the same way Kat did, and Seth nearly grinned. "But clearly she should've listened to me. You see what he did to her!"

The girl frowned. "Or I guess you didn't—well your friends saw! She should've listened to me! She told those jerks that I could get them enough money to leave the city, and they threatened to hurt my sister if I didn't do it."

"The baby." Seth nodded. "So, you did what they wanted…"

"Well sort of…they wanted me to take all of it, but I tried to make it look like I had to do it little by little. The guy was cute, but he was an idiot. He believed me. I was stalling for time. He would've either killed us or taken us with him, so I could get him more money later, and I was trying to figure out how to get rid of him."

"That was smart the way you added yourself as an account holder. The password was the last clue I needed to figure out who you were," said Kat with a proud grin. "You got through my firewall and figured out my password!"

"It's just his name," admitted the girl with a nod in Seth's direction. "It wasn't hard to figure out once I knew who you guys were. As soon as I realized you were shifters, I knew you'd come after me, so I had to make sure you knew who I was too."

Seth was momentarily surprised that Kat's password was his name. After all, he'd assumed she hadn't cared about him much at all until recently, but even disassociated from her cat, she'd still been trying to get back to him, even if she hadn't realized it. His heart swelled with love for his mate, and he barely resisted the urge to stare at her like a lovesick teenager.

"You did good. I'm impressed," admitted Seth, his focus on the girl once more. "Lyndra, is it?"

She nodded. "So you're not mad at me?"

"Under the circumstances, I think you did what you needed to. Money comes and goes, but someone special like you doesn't come around every day. Do you have any family left who are missing you?"

"We fox shifters mostly keep to ourselves. We don't have packs or prides, or whatever the rest of you do," admitted Lyndra with a shrug. "But your alpha did offer to help us...at least until we felt like leaving. Honestly, I could use a break though. Taking care of Ema is harder than you'd think considering how little and cute she is."

Seth grinned. "I hope you stick around for a while. Kat could use a friend who's as good at computers as you are."

"Maybe you can teach her a few things," teased Luc.

Kat rolled her eyes. "Yeah, yeah, so I was outsmarted by a thirteen-year-old. I'm not a bit ashamed." She grinned at the girl. "You're a worthy opponent."

Lyndra nodded, and her big brown eyes grew solemn. "What about Celina?"

"We're gonna do everything we can to get her back…maybe with you and Kat working together we'll have a better chance of tracking her down," explained Seth, not wanting to admit that her sister might already be long gone, or worse.

"Yeah…maybe." Lyndra yawned. "I should check on my sister. Thanks for not being mad."

"I'll take them to see Lacy while we figure out what to do about the other one," volunteered Luc softly.

Seth nodded. "Meet back here in the morning. There isn't much we can do tonight if our hackers don't get any sleep." He winked at Kat, who rolled her eyes once more. She was grinning though, and her smile was everything he never knew he wanted.

Seth waited to hear the sound of the front door closing as Luc and the girl left then turned his attention back toward his mate. "I hate to say it—"

"Then don't. Not until we know for sure. There's no use getting everyone upset until we know. I'll work on hacking into the surveillance outside the apartment. If we get an idea of which direction they went, maybe I can follow them through facial recognition."

Seth didn't even try to pretend he knew what she was talking about.

"Cellphones, stoplights, stores…" Kat listed a few of the many options she'd have. "I can at least see where he took her and get the guys on the scent."

"You can do that?"

Kat smirked. "It'll take me more than a couple hours, but I think I can get us on the trail at least."

"You need to sleep…"

"I will. Later. After I check the apartment building's surveillance."

"Kat…"

Katrina gave him an exasperated look. "The longer this takes, the farther they get with her. The longer she's with them, the less likely we'll be able to save her. We need to move fast. Once I've got an idea of how to find them, Lyndra should be able to help."

"Lyndra is thirteen," protested Seth. He still hadn't completely wrapped his mind around how the tiny fox had hacked into Kat's bank account.

"Lyndra burned through my firewalls and quietly transferred twenty grand into an unknown account, which I've still yet to find. I'm sure she'll be willing to give it back, but that's beside the point. That kid is a genius. Don't underestimate her."

Seth nodded. Kat was right. Even if he still couldn't see Lyndra as a thief who'd stolen a decent chunk of the pride's money, he knew Kat had a point. Together, those two could do anything. He was just glad they were on his side.

****

Katrina worked long into the night, after Seth had finally fallen asleep. She'd been hot on the trail of the wolves but had yet to locate them when she'd finally passed out just as the birds were beginning to herald the rising sun.

When she came to, it was to a giggling thirteen-year-old sitting on the end of the bed, Kat's laptop in her lap and her tiny black painted nails firing away at the keyboard. She was giggling as Seth told her a joke.

"Did you find her?" gasped Katrina, suddenly wide awake. She sat bolt upright, and Seth's hand immediately began to massage her aching back.

"No, but we're getting close. You did a great job last night," chirped Lyndra with a proud grin. "I hope you'll teach me some of this. Most of what I can do involves guessing passwords and codes. You hacked into security cameras, trail cams, and even some store surveillance. I can practically follow them without even leaving this room."

"I didn't mean to fall asleep," huffed Katrina, annoyed with herself for having fallen victim to exhaustion.

"You were tired," said Seth softly, his hand still stroking her back lovingly.

"Yeah…we wouldn't have been able to get her back anyway. They're on pack territory. We have to go through the local alpha," announced Lyndra.

"Which one?" demanded Katrina.

"Uh, South?"

Katrina tried to remember which alpha they'd need to confront.

Seth's hand on her back froze. "South?" He sighed. "Of course, it's those bastards. I bet they're from Milligan's pack. That asshole has been making rogue hunting a pain in the ass for years."

"So?" Lyndra shrugged. "You have an alpha. Just have him contact him."

"He's the kind of guy who will demand payment for permission to hunt on his land. He always does."

"You have plenty of money. I already transferred

the 20k back," said Lyndra quickly.

"If the guys who took your sister told Milligan what you can do, he'll demand more than money. And if he knows how much you had already stolen, he'll want those funds also," explained Seth gently.

"He'll demand twenty thousand *and* want Lyndra too," gasped Katrina in shock. "No, absolutely not!"

"Of course, we're not giving him Lyndra," growled Seth. "But the money?"

Katrina shrugged. "Considering we didn't think we were getting it back to begin with, I have no doubt my dad will trade the twenty thousand for Celina." She knew she was right. She didn't even have to call her dad to ask.

"Then instead of paying him to let us fish my sister out of his woods. Why don't we just pay him to give her back?" asked Lyndra.

"That might work," admitted Seth.

"Maybe…" Katrina bit her lip thoughtfully as she ran through the possibilities. "We'll need my dad to get him on the phone so we can make a deal. This wolf doesn't sound like someone who will talk to just any of us."

"He won't," agreed Seth. "I tried to talk to him a couple years ago when the team wanted to track a rogue onto his territory, but his beta wouldn't even acknowledge us. I had to have my dad confirm, just to get the alpha on the phone to talk to your dad. The guy is a grade A asshole."

Katrina sighed. "Then I'll text my dad. But first, let's make sure that's where they're at. I don't want to have to talk to this guy if they're not there."

"Oh, they're there…and if the feed I just tapped

into from this trail cam is anything to go by, this just got way worse," muttered Lyndra. She spun the laptop around so Katrina could see the screen, and what she saw was absolutely and horribly heartbreaking.

Chapter Nine

"I know who he is." Ward sighed as he stared at the laptop screen. "And he knows who we are."

Katrina stared at her father, her hands on her hips as she awaited his assessment. "Well? Can he do that?"

"Legally? Of course not! But we don't abide by human laws, and shifter laws are…meh." He crossed his arms as he continued to stare at the laptop. "I don't think we have much choice but to give him what he wants."

"That's a lot of money," gasped Dezra.

Katrina glanced at her sister and her mate. Klyn was holding her comfortingly as if it where their own child on the screen being held hostage. Dezra held baby Ema in her arms and was feeding her a bottle, but she looked just as terrified as Katrina felt.

Milligan had somehow known they were watching him. He'd killed the young wolves who'd taken Celina hostage and now held her himself, along with a sign that read his demands. When Katrina's father had called to speak with the alpha, he'd confirmed what Katrina and Seth had assumed. The wolf who'd taken Celina had at one time been in Milligan's pack, but Milligan had kicked him and three other wolves out on their own, leaving them desperate for money and a place to live. They'd been squatting under the bridge when poor clueless Celina had come along. She thought she was attracting a suitor, but she'd played right into their hands and given her family up on a silver platter.

The wolves had taken advantage of her and used

Lyndra to get them enough cash to leave the district, but Lyndra had never transferred them the money, and when Seth had sent his team after them, they'd ran back to their former alpha looking for protection.

Now Milligan was offering Celina back in exchange for half a million dollars, which was significantly more than Lyndra had stolen to begin with.

"That's everything we have in the account, plus some! I'll have to transfer money from another fund," gasped Katrina in shock. "He can't do that!"

"We're lucky he's not claiming her as forfeit. She's a young female close to breeding age. He'd be well within his rights," admitted Ward with a heavy sigh. He ran his hand through his hair and down the front of his face. "We'll just have to give him the money."

"Dad—" Dezra's voice was filled with desperation. "If we clean out the account, we won't have anything for the guys to hunt with. That's every bit of money Kat has made on her paintings and everything I've profited on the houses. Funds to go for repairs on the school and housing for any new pride members. That's everything Nia has contributed all year! You can't seriously just agree to this! We'll be broke."

"Being an alpha means making the hard choices, Dezra, and I can't in good conscious let that asshole keep a teenage girl when we have the money to save her. He's only asking for cash. It could be worse."

Katrina nodded. Her father was right. It was only money. They could always get more. "Seth's team doesn't hunt from the account. They use their own percentages. We can still hunt rogues, and they will earn more money. I can paint more. It'll be rough for a bit, but we can do this." She swallowed anxiously, knowing Seth would agree if he'd been able to get out of bed to join the group meeting.

"What about the school?" whispered her mother. "They need a new water heater, and that's just one of the things on the list of requests. We have several members needing additions and repairs. Nia's bar needs repairs too."

"We'll have enough to keep paying member benefits, so they'll have enough to live on, but that'll be it until we can build our accounts back up," admitted Katrina slowly. "And once Dezra and I make some sales, things will improve, but we should consult the rest of the pride."

"What if they don't think she's worth it?" whispered Dezra tearfully.

"Then they don't belong in this pride anyway," announced Ward. "The kind of people we take care of are not the kind of people who would turn away from someone in need when they have the means to help. I'd rather know now if there are people in our pride who don't share the same heart, because those are potential threats to our way of life, and I believe that we as a pride have a pretty damn good life."

Katrina nodded. "Let me call Seth. As your next alpha, we should hear his opinion too."

Ward nodded. "Does that mean he wants the job?"

"We haven't had a chance to talk about it, but I think you were right to ask him. Ultimately, the choice is his. I'll support whatever he decides," announced Katrina. She dialed his number from her cellphone and waited for him to pick up.

"Kat?" His voice came on the line, and his tone

soothed her immediately. It didn't matter what she had to give up. As long as she had him, she would donate every dime in her personal account and not regret a penny of it.

"We have a possible solution…we want you to hear it and give your input before we convene Dad's council for opinions."

"Okay…" He sounded unsure.

Katrina hit the speaker button so everyone would be able to hear Seth's response as she laid it all out for him. "You were right. The guys who took Celina are Milligan's boys. He killed them, and now he's demanding half a million dollars in exchange for her. We have the money…but it's everything we have. All we'll have left is enough to keep the pride fed and housed, but nothing else. At least until Dezra and I make sales and you're back on the hunt. Everything else, like repairs, will have to wait. What do you think?"

She held her breath, waiting as Seth processed what she'd just told him. She was sure she already knew what his answer would be, but there was always a chance that he wasn't the guy she thought he was. It would break her heart if he wasn't willing to save the girl, but she had absolute faith that he would be just as willing as she was.

"And giving him what he wants is our only option? We're not willing to just go in and kick his ass?"

Katrina hid a smile. "We could…but innocent people will die, and they might kill Celina if they know we're coming. The safest thing for everyone is to just give him the money."

"But does his pack really want him leading them?

We might be doing them a favor if we just kill him instead."

"None of them have asked for our help unseating their alpha. We have to assume they're happy with him and will fight at his command. We can go to war with his pack, but people will die. The wolves outnumber us five to one, and even if we are better fighters, they're better when it comes to rallying other local packs. Cats aren't as easy to collect considering how small our numbers are and how hard it is for us to reproduce," admitted Ward. "As my lead enforcer and possible alpha, what would you do?"

Seth sighed. "Give him the damned money. It isn't worth losing innocent lives. Our people will understand—if they don't, they can leave."

Katrina grinned and turned the speaker off. "I'll be home as soon as I can. Love you." She waited for his response and disconnected the call.

"In the meantime, what are we doing with the fox babies?" asked Dezra as she rocked Ema.

"They're staying with us. They have nowhere else to go and no one to take care of them," answered their mother confidently.

Katrina's heart was overflowing with love for her family, and she was nearly in tears hours later when the council finally dispersed to spread the message among the pride. Like their alpha and Seth, Varg and the others had agreed that forking over their life savings was the right thing to do and that they were sure the rest of the pride would agree.

It warmed Katrina's very soul that the people she called family were so willing to sacrifice for someone they'd never even met. She was on her way home where Seth was patiently awaiting the final decision when thoughts of a happily ever after were interrupted by the distinct scent of wolves. Her gaze searched the area as she came to a stop just outside her own house. She walked a few feet to Varg's front door, and that's when she saw them, four males running at top speed directly toward her. In a flash she shifted and was prepared to run, when one of the males—still in human form—shot her and everything went dark.

****

"*What?*" Seth snarled as he forced himself out of bed, ignoring the flash of pain as his ribs protested the sudden movement. "What the hell do you mean, they took her? Who took her? Who the hell is that damned stupid?!"

Luc held out his hands defensively. "We have three teams going after the wolves right now. Seth, you need to calm down and get back in bed before you hurt yourself."

"A bunch of mangy wolves kidnapped my mate, and you're telling me to calm down? Have you lost your damned mind?" Seth gasped in pain as he stumbled to the end of the bed. "I just convinced her to be with me! I will not lose her." He struggled to make it to his closet and fell to his knees as he felt one of the fractured ribs stab into his lungs. His heart hurt so much more than his ribs in that instant, but he couldn't make his body cooperate. If it had just been his ribs, he would've been on his feet, gritting his teeth through it, but a newly punctured lung would not allow him to soldier through.

Tears sprang to his eyes as he realized he might in fact lose his mate, and he inhaled a deep painfilled breath. "I can't lose her," he wheezed. "Not again."

"I know, Seth. Come on. Let me help you back to bed. We will find her, I swear." Luc's voice was meant to be soothing, Seth knew, but all he could hear was a rushing in his ears. He couldn't even imagine the next day without her, let alone the rest of his life. He wasn't marked. He could live without her physically, but mentally? He nearly sobbed as Luc forced him to his feet and back onto the bed.

"If she dies…" His throat threatened to close on the words. "I refuse to live without her, Luc. I won't do it, not for you or anyone else."

Luc nodded comfortingly. "I know, Seth. She will be fine. She's a smart girl."

"Those bastards threatened to kill a child for half a million dollars…if they have any idea what Kat can do—" His heart threatened to explode out of his chest at the thought. "I can't just lie here!"

"You don't have a choice," growled Luc. "If you die, so does she. She's marked—you're not! Keep your ass in bed, and I will get your girl back. I've waited too damned long to see you two together to miss it now. We aren't going down like this."

Seth groaned. He lay in the bed, uncaring if Luc saw his tears, and he pleaded desperately with every deity he'd ever learned of to keep Kat safe. "Bring her back, Luc." His voice cracked, and he closed his eyes in despair.

He'd never in his entire life felt so helpless and, much as he hated it, he knew Luc was right. If he risked his life to save her, she would die anyway. Her only chance was if Seth stayed exactly where he was and let his friends and family go after her. It went against every instinct he had, and his cat was nearly insane with rage, but Seth didn't have a choice. Katrina needed him to be smart and stay alive.

"I'll get Gossom and Lennix, and I'll call you when I find her. Keep your phone on and charged. You'll be the first one she wants to talk to when I get her back."

Seth nodded. He wanted to thank his friend, but he couldn't force a response through his lips. She'd only been gone an hour, and already he felt like his world was ending.

Footsteps bound up the stairs, and Seth groaned when he smelled his father's uniquely familiar scent.

"I don't need a damned babysitter," he snarled.

"Yes, you do. I know you. You're going to do everything in your power to get out of this bed again and go after her, and I can't let you do that. Varg will make sure you're still alive when I bring Kat back," snapped Luc. "Just lie there and wait, Seth. I promised I'd bring her back, and I will."

"Alive," hissed Seth desperately as Luc rushed out of the room, leaving Varg in charge of Seth's sanity.

****

Luc cursed as he sped through the streets of his alpha's territory. He couldn't admit to Seth that his own heart had been beating out of his chest for the last hour. He liked Katrina, and not in a way that would threaten Seth's claim over her, but in a way that Luc felt like she was practically his sister. He'd only ever cared about one other female that way, and Lennix was currently sleeping with her. He knew exactly where his brother would be because Lennix had been relieving his hunting high not at Nia's bar, but with Nia herself.

Nia was a newcomer to the pride. Team two had rescued her from an abusive pride only a year earlier, and Ward had offered her the bar as an incentive to remain with them where she'd be safe. She trusted almost no one, and she wore body spray to hide her natural scent, but Lennix had gravitated to her instantly. Nia seemed to understand Lennix more than anyone, including Lacy, who was Lennix's therapist.

If Lennix wasn't at Nia's, Luc would be damned surprised. As it was, he pulled into Nia's drive just in time to see Lennix stalk out of her house and slam the door shut behind him. Nia didn't come running after him, but Lennix didn't seem to care. He looked up, saw the SUV, and immediately headed for them.

"Wanna talk about it," asked Luc as his brother slid into the passenger seat and slammed the door.

"Drive," snarled Lennix. "Fast."

"Katrina was kidnapped," blurted Gossom from the backseat.

Lennix growled low. "Seth?"

Luc snorted. There was no way to describe a man who thought he was losing his mate. Desperate? Dangerous? There were many things Seth would be if he lost Kat but none that Luc could say in that instant. "Pissed." Was as close as he could get to an accurate response.

"Good. So am I. Let's go beat some wolf ass." Lennix's voice was low and full of promise, and quite frankly a bit scary to Luc who'd only ever seen his brother in this state of mind one other time—a night he'd just as happily forget if he could.

"What's the plan?" whispered Gossom cautiously.

"There is no plan. We're going after the alpha's

daughter," stated Luc. Typically, that meant guns blazing. Dezra and Katrina had always been Ward's top priority aside from Sammara—his own mate. The entire pride understood that. *Every* otherkin in the realm had the same priorities. There was a sort of hierarchy when it came to who the enforcers protected, and nearly everyone had the same idea. The alpha, their mate, and their children. Half the time one of said offspring was the next alpha but, in this case, she was the next alpha's mate, which made her just as important. Going after an alpha's child was about the same as declaring war. There would be blood.

"No," snapped Lennix, his gaze burning as he stared out the windshield. "We're going after Seth's mate. He's waited too damned long to lose her now. He deserves his mate."

"Seth's mate," agreed Gossom softly.

"Seth's mate," repeated Luc with a nod, and his grip on the steering wheel tightened.

****

"You idiots!" Milligan paced the length of his living room furiously. "What would possess you to kidnap their alpha's daughter? Have you lost your damn minds?" He stared at the four dumbasses who'd taken it upon themselves to kidnap one of the pride cat's females.

She was pretty enough as far as female shifters went and definitely would've been worth keeping if she wasn't a damned alpha's *daughter*! It was bad enough that he was sitting on a female fox, whom the cats desperately wanted back. He'd already taken a risk demanding money in exchange for her life, but now he had their precious female as well. This would not go over well.

"You're so dead," snarled the female in question.

Milligan stared at the woman with bright green feline eyes. The curvy hell cat was pissed. Normally, he'd enjoy that sort of thing, but not with someone whose claws were bigger than his. She'd likely rip his face off if he got anywhere near her. From his experience, the cats trained their females as aggressively as they trained their males. It was fortunate his stupid pack mates had the forethought of tranquilizing her before they'd leashed her in chains and tossed her into the back of an unmarked van. It would've served them right if she'd busted free and slaughtered them all right then and there, but he couldn't get that lucky. Instead, now he had a female fox *and* a female cat, neither of which he wanted anywhere near him.

As a rule, he avoided foxes, not because they were any type of opponent, but they tended to creep him out. He never could decide if they were cats or dogs, and he was a sucker for superstitions, which meant there was always the possibility that they possessed more skill than the average shapeshifter. Milligan subscribed to his own legends and had taken great pride in being a wolf, even going so far as to considering himself superior to the cats, but there were some creatures that he just did not mess with on principle, and the fox, raven, and coyotes were among those he'd rather avoid.

Had the vicious little feline been anyone but the alpha's daughter, he would've taken great pleasure in destroying her, but even he understood that their alpha would not take this lightly. Milligan had two choices. He could contact the alpha, explain the mistake, and give her back before they attacked, and hope they didn't hold it against him, or he could use her. He glanced at the fox and considered how much money he was about to make off of her. They'd agreed to half a million for a female that wasn't even theirs...what would they give for one that was?

"Get out, all of you," Milligan snarled viciously at the four males who'd brought him the female cat. He would've preferred to kill them, just like the last two idiots who'd come running back with their tail between their legs, but as it was, he was confident that a bunch of pissed off cats were well on their way to confront him, and he needed every wolf in his arsenal if he had any hope of getting out of this alive.

"Okay, cat...I know your daddy is sending his feline death squad to get you back, so here's the deal. I get the half a million, and you convince your daddy to call off his cats, or I'll kill the little fox. Do we have an understanding?"

The female hissed—actually hissed at him! Milligan flashed his own fangs and slapped the woman across the face. How dare she disrespect him! His wolf howled furiously, and he considered slitting her throat right then and there, but common sense won out. She had to be alive when the cats came, or they'd slaughter his entire pack. Much as Milligan would like to kill a good number of his own pack mates himself—they were nothing but a bunch of hybrid half breeds after all—he needed them alive. He'd played the lone wolf game once and found it lacking.

Being one of the only full-blooded wolves in his pack meant he was the only alpha. There was no one to challenge him, and all the weak mutts in his pack were too afraid to contradict him. Milligan liked his current position very well. He had all the females he could want and enough males to make sure no one else got any stupid ideas. They kept his territory free of intruders and kept him safe from any other alphas who might think to take his pack. It was good to be king.

"Rot in hell, you evil bastard," snapped the feline.

Milligan snorted. "Poor kitty cat. Someone forget to feed you this morning?"

The woman's gaze shifted from human to feline, and for an instant Milligan regretted taunting her. He'd always heard that the cats were vicious when it came to their enemies. They were more cunning, with sharper teeth and claws, and they were used to hunting in the dark where Milligan and his pack were half blind without the moon's glow to guide them. It was eerie seeing the woman's eyes change as if she were about to shift, but he knew she couldn't so long as he kept her leashed in the silver chains. She was strong, but not strong enough to break them without help. On his own, Milligan would've never been stupid enough to take on a cat, but with a pack at his back? He grinned spitefully. This cat didn't stand a chance.

"Call off your hunting party, or the fox dies." Milligan stomped toward the teenage girl who was still half passed out since he'd tranq'd her hours earlier. He'd made sure the dose was strong enough that she wouldn't be waking up any time soon, and now he almost wished he hadn't. If she cried, maybe the cat would give in.

Milligan lifted the fox up off the floor and held a blade to her throat where her pulse throbbed weakly.

The cat glowered at him. "You took my phone,

stupid."

Milligan heaved a frustrated sigh and dropped the fox on the floor as if she were nothing more than dirty laundry. She moaned but didn't wake up from her drug induced slumber. Not at all like the Alpha's daughter who'd come awake snarling within minutes after arriving inside his house.

"Here." Milligan snatched the cellphone he'd confiscated from the feline off his kitchen table and hit the power button. "Password?"

The woman didn't respond, and Milligan couldn't contain the urge to hit her once more. He smelled blood and grinned victoriously when she spit toward his feet. She had a few bruises now, and a busted lip, but she was otherwise unharmed, a condition he could rectify easily if she didn't start cooperating.

"Password?"

****

Katrina had felt guilty after killing the rogue. She'd looked at his life like a loss. In her mind, he'd once been someone's friend—someone's brother, son, or boyfriend even. Losing control to the dark residue that plagued most otherkin's mind was not a dishonor. It was a tragedy, and the acts committed during those stark moments where not held against the rogue. It was a mercy for the hunters to dispatch their bodies so that their souls could be reincarnated.

There was only one way as far as Katrina knew to save a rogue's mind, and for that they'd need an Omega. However, Omegas were so rare that Katrina had never even met one. She also knew that it was no easy feat for an Omega to save a rogue, and so the hunters continued granting rogues mercy through death, so that their soul could be recycled for another chance at reuniting with their mate, which was the ultimate goal for most.

This wolf was no rogue however, and Katrina would feel no remorse if she was able to get her hands on him. He deserved to pay for what he'd done—not just to Celina, but what he'd done to his pack as well. She'd seen them cowering in the shadows outside his house as they'd carted her into a beautiful log cabin with every possible amenity she could imagine—while they lived in squalor. They were skittish and wild, their eyes betraying their terror. They'd stared at her from decrepit hovels not daring to get any closer. She knew almost nothing about this pack, but she knew wolves in general did not act like kicked dogs in most situations. This man had destroyed these people and tormented them to the point of desperation.

Whatever happened to the man who dared call himself an alpha would be karma, even if Katrina had to be the one to dish it out herself. She'd never cared for the hunting process overall, much preferring her computer skills and painting talents over learning to slice and dice an enemy, but in this instance she and her cat were in agreement. He needed to be dealt with. All those months spent spying on Seth were going to come in handy again…just as soon as she got out of these damned chains.

"Password?" Milligan knelt in front of her once more. He held her phone in his meaty palm, his gaze daring her to deny him yet again. He had a temper on him, and he expressed it readily, but Katrina was a cat, and she could handle a little pain.

"Bitch—"

A knock sounded at the door, interrupting Milligan's implied threat.

"What," snarled her unwanted host viciously as he turned his attention on the man who'd entered his house.

Katrina honestly felt sorry for whoever had interrupted his tirade. She'd seen what he'd done to the assholes who'd kidnapped Celina to begin with, on camera, and she didn't wish that on even her worst enemy. Unless that enemy was Milligan, of course.

"There are f-f-f-four cats circling the p-p-p-perimeter, and f-f-f-four more demanding to speak with you," stuttered the terrified male wolf.

Katrina's heart broke for the man who'd kidnapped her right out from under her family's nose. It was no wonder he was so afraid if he'd been having to deal with Milligan most of his life. She'd be a mess too if her alpha had beat the shit out of her on the daily.

"Their Alpha?"

"No, S-s-s-s-sir!"

Milligan growled wolfishly and twisted back to face Katrina once more. "Daddy must not love you as much as you think, princess." He smirked and smashed her phone on the floor, then stomped on it for good measure. He whipped out his own phone, and Katrina watched as he pressed a series of numbers onto the on-screen dial pad. The phone rang once, and her father's voice was immediately on the other line.

"You dumbass—"

"Hush now, kitty. I have your precious princess, and she's fine—mostly. Right, princess?" Milligan stared threateningly in her direction, daring her to defy him. "Be a good girl and tell your daddy that you're fine."

Katrina hissed once more. "This is not going to end well for you, wolf. I guarantee it."

Milligan snorted dismissively. "See, she's fine. Still has her tongue and everything. I'm ready to negotiate. I figure you were willing to pay for the fox. You must be willing to do a bit more for your precious kitten."

"We have your money, Milligan. We agreed to the deal!"

Katrina grimaced. Her father sounded so strong and alpha, but she could hear the pain in his voice. He was afraid.

"You did, but now I have two of your females." Milligan paced the length of the living room as if their current situation was merely a business deal. "And this one is so much more…interesting than the other." He grinned malevolently and winked at Katrina.

"She's already mated."

"So?" Milligan rolled his eyes, and Katrina made a mental vow to never roll her eyes ever again. She wanted to be nothing like this monster.

"So, he will slaughter your entire pack if you don't let her go. He's my lead enforcer and not someone you want to mess with, Milligan."

Katrina knew Seth would not be coming to her rescue any time soon, but she also knew her father was right. The instant Seth was able, he'd be tearing down this wolf's door and demanding blood. Seth was not merely a well-trained hunter, he was her mate, and the one man more desperate to see her safe than her own father.

"There are eight felines outside my territory

circling like vultures, and none of them seem like a lead enforcer, so unless her pitiful mate has decided she's not worth his time, then your big bad kitty cat isn't here, and since he wasn't among the first to arrive, I can only assume he won't be joining the party. Why—doesn't really matter to me. Just know that I see your lame threat and do you one better. Call off your hunters and back off or I will kill the fox."

There was no sense arguing Seth's love for her. This was a man who could never understand such a thing, and they all knew it. Instead, her father went straight for the throat. "Kill the fox, and every cat outside your door will attack."

"All they'll get is a bunch of flea-bitten bastards. I'm safe in my den where your cats will never touch me. My pack will defend me with every bit of breath in their body. They know what'll happen if they fail."

Katrina watched the stuttering male who'd kidnapped her fidget nervously. He wasn't nearly as loyal as Milligan claimed, but he was terrified. Every once in a while, he'd glance at her, then look away anxiously. She hoped that meant he was having second thoughts about having kidnapped her and might be convinced to set her free, so that she could rid him and his pack of their current alpha.

"Pity you chose to rule with fear rather than lead by example. Your time is about up, Milligan, and if my boys don't kill you, your pack will. Best to quit while you're ahead. You hand over my daughter and the fox, and I'll give you your damned money. No one has to die tonight."

Katrina doubted Milligan read into her father's offer the way she did. If he had, he never would've agreed.

"I hand your females over and you walk away?"

"I need an account number to transfer the money, Milligan. No tricks."

Katrina watched the wolf consider her father's offer. He was a damned fool, and the man who'd kidnapped her knew it too. Soon enough, Milligan was ordering him to cart her and the teenage fox to their territory border where Katrina's pride mates were waiting to rescue her. Whatever Milligan expected to happen, however, was not what his pack mate had in mind. After the wolf exited with the fox, he returned to grab Katrina But the instant he'd carried her from the house, he dropped her at the end of the long porch and then whispered in her ear.

Chapter Ten

"Don't kill me."

For half a second, Katrina had no clue what he meant, but then her chains were falling to the ground around her, and he was sprinting off the porch and into the forest leaving her alone.

The door to Milligan's home was now closed, but Katrina was free, and one solid wood plank was all that was stopping her from giving him exactly what he deserved.

She considered the fox who remained asleep. She could scoop the girl up and deliver her to the border where the pride would help them both to safety, but then Milligan would have her family's money, and he would still be alive. She warred with her conscience for a moment, considering how Seth would feel, but how Seth felt about her storming into the house to murder the bastard wolf was not the same thing Seth himself would do if he were in her situation.

Seth might've preferred for Katrina to get herself and the girl to safety, but had it been him, he'd be in the house delivering justice. She reminded herself that she wasn't trained, but given the way Milligan's pack cowered from him, she doubted they would interfere on his behalf.

It might be the stupidest thing she'd ever done, or it might save an entire pack of terrified wolves, but either way, Milligan only understood one thing, and while she typically did not condone violence, Katrina knew she couldn't just walk away.

She'd made it halfway across the porch when a familiar male voice interrupted her approach.

"Katrina, no!"

"I have to, Luc. He doesn't deserve to live," she whispered back. Katrina didn't turn to look at her new friend. She couldn't. She knew if she did, he'd change her mind.

"Seth needs you!"

"I didn't mark him. He will be all right."

"He won't, and you know it! He will not survive if you get yourself killed! I promised to bring you back, and that's damn well what I'm going to do. Get your ass down here!"

Katrina flinched. Luc was right, but that didn't detract from Milligan's offenses. "Luc—"

"No, Katrina. Seth will never forgive either of us. Get. Down. Here!"

Katrina spun to scowl at Luc just as the front door flew open and Milligan raced out, a blade in his hand at the ready.

"Katrina!" Luc's voice was filled with terror as Milligan snatched Katrina in his arms and pressed the blade to her throat.

"Never trust a cat," muttered Milligan angrily. He held Katrina hostage against his body, the blade piercing her skin and drawing blood. She didn't dare move for fear of slicing her own throat.

"Take your fox and go, feline. The princess and I need to have a little chat."

Milligan started to back toward his own door.

"Damn it, Kat!" Luc bounded up the stairs.

"Get back," bellowed Milligan, and his blade sank just a fraction deeper. It burned, but Katrina would rather die than let Milligan get his hands on her again.

"I can't leave without her," snapped Luc.

"Too damned bad. She should've left when she had the chance," snapped Milligan angrily.

"I know!" Luc cursed. "And I agree. But if you let me have her, I'll take her out of here kicking and screaming. She won't lay a hand on you, I swear!"

"Bullshit!" Milligan backed a little farther across the porch. "If I let her go, I'll have *two* cats on my ass. The only way you're going to go is if I keep this one. Take the fox while I'm still feeling generous and *leave*."

"Actually, you'll have four cats on your stupid ass," hissed a second familiar voice, and Katrina watched in surprise as Lennix and Gossom appeared from the tree line behind Luc. "We're not going anywhere without our princess." He winked at Katrina, who could've cried in relief at the sight of them.

"I have a blade to her throat. I can decapitate her faster with this blade than you can make it up those stairs. If you have any brain at all in those stupid, thick-headed skulls, I suggest you back the hell up!"

"They're not stupid," exclaimed Katrina, and before she could think better of it, she shoved her elbow into the wolf's ribs hard enough to crack the protective bones guarding his heart and lungs.

Milligan gasped in pain and dropped the blade at her feet, where Katrina promptly snatched it up and twisted to face him.

"Katrina...no. Not like this," whispered Luc.

"You're not a killer."

"Consider it karma," huffed Katrina, and she reached up to wipe away the little bit of blood Milligan had drawn while holding her hostage. It still stung, but she knew the wound would be healed long before she even made it home. Thankfully, Seth would never see it.

"Not you, Katrina." This time it was Lennix's voice, and he sounded so much more desperate than his brother had.

"Our alpha promised to let him live another night," reminded Gossom quietly.

Katrina swore. "My father—"

"Is our alpha," reminded Gossom. "If we don't keep our word, we're no better than this guy."

Much as she detested him for it, Gossom was right. "Fine," she snarled as she tossed the blade down behind her. She should've walked away then, but one look at the unconscious Celina had her leaping onto the gasping wolf and pounding her fists into his face until Luc and Lennix could pull her away.

"See? I told you I'd take her out of here kicking and screaming," muttered Luc as he lugged Katrina away from the groaning wolf.

"Now's your chance," cried Katrina.

"We said we'd leave him—" began Gossom once more.

"Not you," hissed Katrina as the wolves Milligan called his pack began to emerge from the forest.

"Shit…we should go," whispered Lennix .

Gossom rushed forward to heft the sleeping fox into his arms, and together the five of them backed away from the cabin where Milligan still lay on the porch gasping for breath.

Milligan snarled at the approaching wolves, promising all matter of pain and revenge, but the wolf pack didn't stop. They circled him like the feral beasts he'd made them, their intent clear.

Katrina wished she could say she regretted giving the wolves the opportunity to relieve themselves of their tormentor, but a second look at the deathly pale teenage girl in Gossom's arms was all the clarity she needed. Whatever the wolves did to him was exactly what he deserved, and she'd live with that for the rest of her life.

"Damn it, Kat," mumbled Luc once more. "Seth is going to be so pissed."

"Seth would have ripped his throat out," snapped Katrina in frustration.

"And if they leave him alive, Seth still might, but that's not the point," insisted Luc as they made their way through the forest, ignoring Milligan's blistering threats.

"Then what is the point? The bastard tortured those poor people. He threatened to murder a child! He was a monster, and he wasn't even rogue! There is no excuse for what he did, and if he'd been human, they would've locked him up and thrown away the key," huffed Katrina. "If the other wolves don't kill him, he'll keep hurting them. He'll hurt other innocent people!"

"I seriously doubt Milligan will be doing anything to anyone ever again, even if they don't kill him," mumbled Gossom.

"The point is that you are my best friend's mate— the love of his damn life, and I have watched him pine after you from the first day he met you. He spent years of his life alone, loyal to you! He waited, and he deserves to be happy, damn it! The only thing he's ever asked me to do in his whole damned life was to bring you home alive, and you nearly got yourself killed! I refuse to tell him he lost his mate because I couldn't keep one little feral feline from sacrificing herself to the greater good. I don't care if Lennix goes back and breaks that damned wolf's neck, but it won't be you," exclaimed Luc.

Katrina balked.

"Really, can I?" asked Lennix with a devious grin.

"Get your ass to the car. All of you," bellowed Luc, clearly fed up with the whole lot of them.

Katrina was safely in the SUV when Luc retrieved his phone from his jean pocket and called the other waiting teams back to Pride territory. She expected him to call her father next, but she was pleasantly surprised when he turned the speaker on and Seth's voice echoed over the line.

"Your princess is safe, Seth," said Luc with a grin, and Katrina promptly burst into tears.

"You made her cry," growled Lennix. "Seth is going to kill you."

Seth laughed with noticeable relief on the other side of the line. "Is she hurt?" he asked.

"Not really...you should see the other guy," chirped Gossom.

Katrina could only manage a mollified blubber at the comforting sound of her mate's voice. She'd thought she'd never see him again when she'd awoken in the wolf's cabin, and she'd been prepared to sacrifice herself to make sure Milligan never hurt anyone else ever again. But now that she was safe and well on her way back home, the idea of seeing Seth again was the most amazing miracle she could imagine.

"Tell him you love him, so I can hang up and get you home," instructed Luc softly.

Katrina laughed through her tears. "I kicked his ass."

Seth's pain-filled groan of laughter filled the speaker, and she grinned in response. "Who'd have known all those months I spent spying on you would save my life, not once, but twice." Katrina laughed shakily. "Get some rest. I'll be home soon—and Seth?"

"Yeah?"

"I love you."

Epilogue

Lyndra could say with complete honesty that no one had ever cared about her as much as the cats seemed to. The alpha and his mate had taken her and her sisters into their home as if they were their own children and made sure they had fresh clean clothes and all the food they could stomach.

Celina hadn't spoken much since waking up, but she spent a lot of time with one of the pride females—a woman by the name of Lacy Baraek who seemed to be making progress with Lyndra's older sister. Lyndra had talked to the woman as well, and while it seemed Lyndra wasn't nearly as traumatized as her sister was, they all agreed that Lyndra would see her once a week for a few months as well.

Ema was doing amazing, and Sammara—Katrina's mom—had thankfully taken over the mothering duties. Lyndra didn't mind, though. Thanks to Sammara, Lyndra was able to attend a real school with other shifters just like her. Granted, they were almost all cats, but they seemed like a nice bunch, and no one had treated her like a silly little fox yet.

Katrina had kept her promise to teach Lyndra the ins and outs of real computer hacking so long as Lyndra pledged not to rob anymore bank accounts, which was an easy enough vow to keep when the cats were providing everything they needed or even wanted.

There were moments when Lyndra missed her parents, but they were similar to the times she'd missed them while they were still alive, and she knew it wouldn't have been long before they disappeared again, maybe returning with yet another baby in tow. Lyndra shuddered to imagine the rest of her life raising her parents' children and was relieved that she had someone to help her now. Much as she loved her sister, Lyndra wanted to be a child like any other thirteen-year-old, and she spent a good amount of time making friends with the local cat population rather than hiding from them as she had in the city. Life was good.

****

Katrina smiled as she hung up the phone and slid it onto the bedside table.

"Can you stop worrying now? You're as bad as Lennix," whined Seth. He flipped onto his stomach and tugged Katrina down next to him, where he pressed his lips against her belly, leaving light butterfly kisses across her tender flesh.

"I just want to make sure they're doing okay," huffed Katrina, but she grinned back at him, and Seth's heart did a little flip. He'd been thanking his lucky stars that she was back in his arms, unharmed, where she belonged for months, and saw no point in stopping now.

"You just walked her home an hour ago. She's fine."

Katrina sighed once more. "Have you heard anything else about Milligan?"

"Still missing, but I doubt he'll ever turn up. The wolves have a new alpha, and she seems like a much better fit. She doesn't appear to mind us tracking rogues through her territory either," explained Seth as he turned his head to lay his ear against Katrina's stomach.

"She's stubborn, like you," whispered Katrina as she reached down to brush Seth's hair away from his face, but she wasn't referring to the wolf pack's new alpha, and they both knew it.

"I think she gets that from you," muttered Seth, and he pressed another kiss to her slightly rounded stomach.

Katrina giggled, and Seth swore it was the most beautiful sound in the world. "Then she had better be as beautiful as you are."

Seth snorted. "If she knows what's good for her, she'll be every bit like her mother."

"Give yourself credit, Seth. You are smart, talented, strong, patient, considerate, and everything a cat should be." She reached down and took his face in her hands. "If she knows what's good for her, she'll be every bit as amazing as you are." Katrina tugged him further up her body until she could press her lips against his. "I love you, Seth Mourgent, so much. Thank you for saving me."

"I love you too, Kat. Thank you, for finally coming home."

A word about the author...

Born in Georgetown, Ohio, Cassidee Meeks finds her home in a small town in Eastern Kentucky where she spends her days with her husband wrangling her kids and all the stray cats her family will allow.

You might find her tending chickens in her backyard or with her nose buried in a good book. Her favorite genre is romance, and she enjoys reading paranormal, sci-fi, historical, and fantasy.

Most days, Cassidee can be found deep in her writing cave where she spends her days arguing with fictional characters, who inevitably get their way and their stories told.

~*~

Please check out Cassidee's first book at TWRP

The Lady and the Wolf

Thank you for purchasing
this publication of The Wild Rose Press, Inc.

For questions or more information
contact us at
info@thewildrosepress.com.

The Wild Rose Press, Inc.
www.thewildrosepress.com